Stormy Acres

May 2011

Buddy,
a great man!
Jammy Huie

Stormy Acres

Tamara Eden Huie

Copyright © 2011 by Tamara Eden Huie.

Library of Congress Control Number:		2011902830
ISBN:	Hardcover	978-1-4568-7378-3
	Softcover	978-1-4568-7377-6
	Ebook	978-1-4568-7379-0

All rights reserved. No part of this book may be reproduced or transmitted in any form or by any means, electronic or mechanical, including photocopying, recording, or by any information storage and retrieval system, without permission in writing from the copyright owner.

This is a work of fiction. Names, characters, places and incidents either are the product of the author's imagination or are used fictitiously, and any resemblance to any actual persons, living or dead, events, or locales is entirely coincidental.

This book was printed in the United States of America.

To order additional copies of this book, contact:
Xlibris Corporation
1-888-795-4274
www.Xlibris.com
Orders@Xlibris.com

DEDICATION

Stormy Acres is dedicated to my father, Thomas J. Eden, who was born at Stormy Acres, the Eden homestead in Monticello, Iowa, in 1917. He helped his father make the farm profitable, and also raised, trained and raced standard-bred horses. He raced at Maywood Park in Chicago, Illinois, Phoenix, Arizona, and trained horses at the Spring Garden Ranch thirty miles outside of Daytona Beach, Florida. He raced at many county fairs in the Mid-West, and was on the Fair Board for the Great Jones County Fair in Monticello. Dad was a kind, generous, witty and handsome man. Everyone liked him. His mottos were: "Be happy," and "Count your blessings." He died in 1986, leaving us with wonderful memories.

1980's

H ERE WE ARE, twenty-one years later, and today is Harrison's birthday. As I sit comfortably in a lawn chair behind the house, I can smell the fresh fragrance of the lilacs that envelop the bushes they hang on. It is a warm day with a soothing cool breeze. I am happy and content with my life.

The near sound of the big green John Deere tractor means that Harrison is back from the field. Harrison is 6'2" tall, and has dark wavy hair, hazel eyes and long black eyelashes. He has a perfect smile, and a personality that draws people to him—especially the young ladies.

As I watch him turn off the tractor and get down on the ground, my thoughts began to drift back t o the first time I saw him, but, now isn't the time for reminiscing.

Harrison is walking towards me. He has on his usual work jeans, a white T-shirt and brown leather work boots. He now owns half of Stormy Acres, and doesn't mind working the long hours it takes to make the farm profitable. He loves farming. He milks thirty cows twice a day, raises chickens, raises and sells hogs, breeds horses and has a dog named Racer.

"Harrison," I asked. "You ready for your birthday cake?"

Taking off his dusty hat, and slapping it hard on a pant leg, he replied, "I've been ready all day!"

1950's

Daddy started the old '39 Ford pick-up; we're on our way to the horse barn at the fairgrounds. I like watching him change gears with the floor shift and hearing the rocks on the gravel road hit the truck with ping ping sounds. He is keeping her at 45 miles per hour. After all, it is only three or four miles into town. Highway 38 is not a busy highway, but everyone in the rural area knows our truck; they wave or honk, or sometimes do both!

It is summer, and the scenery is breathtaking. There are thousands of small colorful wild flowers dotting the countryside. The farms are neatly spread out—the land flat with rich black soil hungry for seed.

Dad is so handsome. I believe he could date any woman in town if he so desired. Everyone likes him; I do too. I adore him. He is 6'2" tall with a head full of black wavy hair. He has gray-blue eyes, smiles, tells jokes and whistles a lot. Once when we passed by the cemetery on the way to town, he asked me if I knew how many dead people are buried in the cemetery. At first, I didn't catch on, and I answered, "I don't know."

"All of them," he said laughing.

Dad has a lot of friends that like to play pranks on each other. One night when dad was bowling in town, some of the men drove his car to another town and parked it at the bowling alley there. They have a lot of fun. We think nothing of leaving our keys in our car, and we don't lock our house doors. Monticello is a safe place to live.

Dad isn't a hunter or a fisherman. When he was much younger, he boxed. Now he likes to play poker, bowls on a league, and is into racing horses.

Thomas John Eden

"Tom"

Chapter 1

1950's

IT IS JUNE, 1957. I am sixteen, and my name is Jane Ahlrichs. Daddy's name is Tom. His grandparents came to this country in the 1800's to farm. From that time, the farm has been called Stormy Acres. Ahlrichs are prosperous farmers.

Even though I can't see into the future, I believe the best time of my life is right now. My girlfriends and I have lots of fun. We love music, we go to dances, we wear black and white saddle shoes, and full skirts with as many can cans that we can get under them. Sometimes we pull our hair back into pony tails, and other times we wear our hair long with the ends curled up. This is a sweet time of innocence, desires and dreams; a time never to be again. I know that, but I'm comfortable living in this façade of stardust, and don't want to believe it will ever be crushed down to make way for a cold capacious way of life. I want things to stay just as they are.

Dad and I parked close to the horse barn, and saw Sharon's jeep. She was there cleaning out stalls. About two years after mom left, and the divorce became final, dad started dating Sharon. Like us, she loves horses. She works in an electrical shop in town, and has two children that live with their father in Cedar Rapids. She has shown me their pictures. They are cute. I'm glad Sharon helps with Stormy, because dad has a lot to do at the farm, and a horse is a lot of work and takes up a lot of time.

Sharon told us that her father has been in prison for robbery. Evidently, he robbed a jewelry store in Des Moines; the salesman was shot in one of his arms as he yelled for help. Sharon's mother then divorced Mr. Williams, and married a man who owns a large farm in the rural area of Manchester.

To me, Sharon looks Hispanic. She has long glossy black hair and pretty dark eyes. Her skin is smooth and tanned, but her maiden name is Williams, and that is English. She is rather pretty. We get along alright, but I can't get close to her like I was to mom before she divorced dad and moved to New York. Dad, I guess, is crazy about Sharon though, so I do my best to be nice to her. She never spends the night at the farm, so if she and dad are having sex, it, most likely is at her apartment.

Chapter 2

I LOVE STORMY Acres. It is hard to imagine anyone else ever living here. One day, dad had the deed out and showed it to me. It was a Mr. John Delahunt, back in 1853 who must have known this spot would be perfect for a farm. Then the land was cleared, the house built and many necessary buildings erected.

After the Delahunt's sold the farm, there were other families who farmed it too. Then, in 1891, my great grandfather bought the farm, and named it Stormy Acres.

Turning off Highway 38, our lane runs about 100 yards from the highway up to our house. About 50 yards to the right of the house is a rocky bluff that stretches up 30 feet from the bottom. We keep hogs in the pasture below the cliff.

Our large three-story house is white with a summer kitchen connected at the bottom level. Outside of it, there is a shower, and then a row of small buildings used for tools, storing wood and smoking meat. We have four bedrooms, a kitchen, living area, two bathrooms, and two large porches.

Our unique furniture was well taken care of and, thankfully, passed down from our ancestors. We have an oak hall tree, and old wooden stand-up record player that we call Victor. It is in dad's bedroom along with a lot of old 33 □'s. Our bedrooms are filled with antique beds, chests and dressers. Sometimes I feel like I live in a museum. I often wonder if Sharon likes the way our home is decorated, and if she would like living here with us. If so, I hoped it would be a long time before that happens; I'm not ready to share Stormy Acres with her. I guess I'm selfish.

Stormy Acres has four hundred acres of rich black soil. She has a lot of old, but sturdy buildings: a haymow, the milking barn, corn bins, oats bins, machine shop, chicken coop, pig pens, silo and buildings for horses. Outside of the cow lot, dad keeps a water trough stocked with catfish. At some point and time someone built a tornado cellar out back of the house. I never go down there—it is dark and scary.

Chapter 3

DAD AND I walked together into the horse barn. Sharon's eyes lit up when she saw us. We exchanged good mornings, and then I picked up a shovel to help her clean the stall. Dad went on down to one of the stalls to check on a horse that belongs to one of his good friends. Then dad put a harness on Stormy, "talked" to her, and brushed her a little. Then he took her over to the track, went through the gate and let her go around the track at her own pace. Dad looked good on the sulky.

There's a race coming up soon in Maquoketa, and I know dad would really like to see Stormy win. The races are great. Sharon and I are both going. Whether we are racing in Maquoketa, or in any other town, before the races start, the drivers always find time to sit around the tack room to gossip and smoke cigars! The horsemen and horsewomen have many good stories to tell; some stories are told over and over! They seem to get better every time they are told. The races are very competitive, and every driver wants his horse to win, but, of course, they don't always win. Most of the drivers are good losers, but every now and then, one will get "hot under the collar" and has to be calmed down.

Chapter 4

IT IS A Saturday night. Dad and Sharon had started on their way to Dubuque, but dad realized the he had left his billfold on his dresser, so they stopped out at the farm to get it. Sharon has on a lovely burgundy-colored dress with a white collar and white sleeves. She is wearing black patent shoes, and has on silver jewelry. She looks nice. Dad looks somewhat like John Wayne, and somewhat like Robert Mitchum with his chocolate-covered slacks and beige pull-over.

Some nights when dad and Sharon go out together, I stay with one of my grandmothers, but this night, I stayed at the farm. Butch, our hired man is here, so I'm not alone. Butch is a large man, quiet-spoken, clean-cut and very neat. He has worked for dad for a long time, and has a great sense of humor like dad. His real name is Robert Benson. He does a lot of work around the farm, is a master carpenter, a good mechanic and helps with Stormy. He has a son named Gary who lived with his maternal grand-parents until he joined the Air Force.

Butch hasn't seen him in a long time. I know he misses him because he talks about him often. He sends money to Gary whenever Gary needs a little extra. He sent money to Gary's grandparents too, before Gary joined the service.

Chapter 5

SUMMERS IN IOWA are hot and dusty. There are heavy rainfalls with howling thunder and quick splashes of lightning. During the hottest months—July, August and September, you can see ripples of heat waves dancing upwards from the streets. For years, we have had a water fountain at the one and only intersection; people line up to drink from it to cool themselves, and to quench their thirst. Driving around the small towns, people are outside mowing their yards, or working in their gardens. Monticello is somewhat of a mundane town, but I feel safe here, and the people are friendly.

During fair week, which is in August, race fans spend afternoons at the race track. There are only three families here that actually participate in the races. I don't think people understand what is involved in having a race horse. You have to love the sport, and be able to afford it and devote yourself to the work and time it entails. I love the races and the carnivals that go along with the races because of the foot-long hot dogs, cotton candy, taffy, and caramel corn. I wait anxiously for nightfall when the entertainment starts. The fireworks that are displayed on the last night of the fair are spectacular.

So often I lie awake thinking about joining a carnival after I graduate. I think about buying a ferris wheel or a scrambler; living in a small trailer; at night the carnies would come to my trailer, sit around to talk about sales and where we will go next.

Chapter 6

WE PULLED INTO the fairgrounds in Maquoketa late Friday. Sharon was with us. After dad got Stormy out of the body of the truck, Sharon and I hosed off the tarp and set up housekeeping. We had cots, chairs, and a small kitchen. Everything we needed, we had.

While dad got Stormy stalled, Sharon began preparing supper. She took the grill outside, lit it and put big juicy hamburgers on it. We had baked beans along with the burgers, and crunchy potato chips. For dessert, she put scoops of strawberry ice cream in large cones for us. I cleaned up after we ate, and Sharon said she was going to walk the midway and look around the fairgrounds. Dad and I set the cots up and watched our small black and white television. Sharon got back about an hour later. Then we laid down on the cots and fell asleep in our blue jeans and shirts.

The three of us woke about 6 a.m. Sharon made coffee and then fried eggs and bacon on the gas stove. It tasted so good. The truck now was beginning to smell like a house instead of horse! "Home away from home."

After breakfast, dad and Sharon left for the barn. It was time to feed and water Stormy. The races didn't start until 1 p.m., so he had plenty of time to warm her by jogging her around the track. I waited awhile, cleaned up the kitchen, and went down to the barn too, to see if there were any other girls my age to pal around with. At the barn, I could feel the excitement in the air.

Stormy raced on Saturday and Sunday. She won on Saturday. Dad was happy about that, and gave me $10.00 to spend on the midway. It was hot and dusty, but we were thankful it wasn't raining. I changed later in the day into pink shorts and a white striped pull-over and wore my tennis shoes. I stopped at the Lions stand and enjoyed a tenderloin; fries and a Pepsi. Then I rode a lot of rides and played some games, but didn't win a thing. My $10.00 had shrunk to $1.50. I was having a great time though I hadn't found anyone to pal around with. I was tired, and decided to go back to the truck to lie down. As I was walking by the Carney trailers, I heard what sounded like a real heated argument. Not wanting to be seen, I dodged behind the back of a camper where I could see and hear better, and not be noticed. I was eavesdropping, but I wanted to know what was going on.

The woman's voice sounded a lot like Sharon's but it couldn't be. Who would she be arguing with in Maquoketa?

"I'm pregnant," I heard her say. "We have to get married."

"Honey, that's your problem, not mine," he said.

"You bastard," she cried out. "I hate you. You've used me. I want the $500.00 I borrowed from Tom that you used for your drug sales!" She was furious, I could tell, and she began to cry.

Then, peeking around the back of the camper, I saw the man grab Sharon by her shoulders, and shake her real hard. He put up his hand like he was going to hit her, but he drew back. I heard him tell her that she had better keep her mouth shut, or else! When Sharon ran from the man, I got a good look at her, and, yes, it was Sharon. It was hard to believe.

If Sharon was pregnant, it wouldn't be long, and the "cat would be out of the bag." I walked back to the truck in a daze knowing that I needed to tell dad about this, and that would be hard to do because he liked her.

Our winnings that weekend in Maquoketa were $850.00. Dad was pleased. Sharon was quiet on the way, and I was very cool to her. Dad didn't seem to realize it. He was happy and whistled most of the way back home. After we unloaded Stormy, and all the equipment, I cleaned out the truck like I always do when we get back home after racing. Sharon made some excuse, and she left. We said "goodbye" to her, and she drove off in her jeep. Dad finished whatever he was doing, and he and I drove back to the farm where Butch was anxiously waiting to hear the results of the races in Maquoketa. Dad told him that Stormy won first place on Saturday, and came in second on Sunday. We left there with $950.00. Butch is pleased.

Chapter 7

WHEN BUTCHS' WIFE Sara died, Butchs' son, Gary, went to Seattle, Washington to live with his maternal grandparents, the Hamiltons. Butch left town for a year or so after working for one of the factories in town for ten years. When he returned to Monticello, he needed a job, and that is when dad hired him, and never regretted it.

Butch remodeled an area in our attic for him, and included a bathroom too. His "apartment" is always neat and clean. He keeps a large colored picture of Gary on his bureau. Butch eats his meals with us, and entertains us with hilarious and bizarre stories. I'm not always sure if they are true, or not, but it doesn't matter.

Chapter 8

EARLY ON WEDNESDAY morning, I heard a loud knock on the kitchen door. Putting on my bathrobe, I rushed down the stairs to see who was there. It was John Boorman, our neighbor. I asked him to come in. I knew by the look on his face, there was something the matter.

"Hi, Janie," he said softly. "Is your dad up?"

Dad had heard the knocking, and John's voice, and wasn't far behind me when John came inside.

"Tom," he said. "I'm sorry. I have terrible news. Sharon is dead."

"Tom," John said, "When Sharon didn't show up for work on Thursday, Karl said he didn't know what to think. He waited until about 1 p.m. that day and went up to her apartment, where he found Sharon laying on the floor." "It looked to him like she had been shot; he assumed she was dead." "Karl told me that he liked Sharon—that she was a good employee. She would go into work early on Friday mornings to finish the billing and work on correspondence, so he could close the office early on Fridays to give his employees a longer weekend."

"Did Karl call the police?" dad asked.

"Yes, he said he did. I thought it strange that Karl hasn't called you, Tom, but I guess he just can't bear talking to you about it knowing how close you and Sharon have been."

Then Butch came downstairs. He had heard the conversation. The three of us stood there looking at John for what seemed like an hour. None of us knew what to do or say. Dad sat down at the table looking distraught, but he held his composure. I think he was in shock.

About half an hour later, Sheriff Wilson drove up our driveway, got out of his patrol car, opened the porch door and came into the kitchen. He saw dad, Butch, and John sitting at the table, and he sat down with them. With sad eyes, the sheriff looked at dad; he could tell we had heard the news as we were all so somber. I went to the stove and fixed coffee for everyone, including sugar, cream and donuts.

The sheriff told us that Sharon had been shot in her apartment, and the coroner had her body.

The men were drinking the coffee I made for them, when the sheriff asked dad if he owned a gun. Dad went upstairs and brought down his rifle. He handed it to the sheriff. The sheriff looked it over and wrote down the serial number, but didn't take it with him when he left. Dad told the sheriff that it was the only gun he owned, and it was to use on unwanted varmints—not human varmints. The sheriff thanked us for the coffee and donuts, got up to leave, and told us he would be in touch.

"Tom," John said. "If there is anything I can do, please call me."

"Thanks," dad said as he walked John to the door.

Chapter 9

I KNEW THERE would never be a right time to tell dad what I had seen in Maquoketa, so I decided to get it over with. After John left, I told dad that I needed to talk to him. He led me into the family room and we sat down. After I blurted out everything I could remember about the man who threatened Sharon, dad thanked me for letting him know. Dad wanted to know if I could recognize the man if I ever saw him again, and I said that I could. Then, dad got up and walked outside. Butch told me not to follow him, that he probably needed some time by himself. I thought so too. Butch went back to work, and I went up to my bedroom.

That night, after the animals had been fed, the cows milked, dad came up to my room and sat down on the bed.

"Janie," he said. "You need to call Sheriff Wilson tomorrow and go see him. He needs to know everything that you told me, as it very well could help him solve the case, and we would know who killed Sharon." I asked God for help in my prayers that night.

Chapter 10

THE NEXT MORNING, I called Sheriff Wilson's office to set up an appointment with him. A woman promptly answered and forwarded my call to him.

"Sheriff Wilson here," he answered. "Can I help ya?"

"This is Jane Ahlrichs," I said. "I have some information that might help you with the investigation concerning Sharon Hanson's death."

"Good, how 'bout two here in my office. That good for you?" he asked.

"Yes, I'll see you at two," I replied, and hung up.

I parked the car in a space close to the front of the Community Building on First Street, got out of the car, put the change in the parking meter, and went into the brick building. Before our appointment, I had put on a blue dress, and tied my hair back in a ponytail with a blue and white ribbon. I thought that if I thought I looked good, I would have more confidence to get through the meeting. I am very shy around adults.

After entering the building, I noticed a large lettered sign on the second door on the left side of the hall. The hall smelled musty I thought; anyway, I knocked on the door with the large lettering which read SHERIFF'S OFFICE, and the sheriff opened the door, greeted me and asked me to sit down; he seemed pleased to see me.

Our sheriff isn't a Rock Hudson, or a picture of neatness. His uniform looked disheveled. He is short, stocky, has bushy eyebrows, and yellow teeth. He is almost bald. I noticed—and had to chuckle to myself—what a mess his desk was in with loose papers all over it and stacks of files everywhere, plus a nasty ashtray. But, Sheriff Wilson is affable and has served our town diligently for many years and he was well-liked. Sheriff Wilson made me feel comfortable, and offered me a stick of Juicy Fruit chewing gum which I readily accepted. Then we got down to business. I told him what I had seen and heard that day in Maquoketa—how the man grabbed Sharon's shoulders, shook her hard and threatened her. I related that Sharon demanded he repay her the $500.00 she had borrowed from dad that the man, evidently had used for his dealings in drugs. I hated to, but I told the sheriff that Sharon told the man she was pregnant, and that they should get married.

The man, I described to the sheriff, was not tall, had curly blond hair, and was wearing a baseball cap turned backwards on his head. He had on a T-shirt with short sleeves rolled up holding a pack of cigarettes in the folds. He had beige-colored cutoffs on, and there was a big ugly green lizard tattoo on his left arm. The sheriff asked if I would be able to recognize the man, and I said that I could.

"Tell your dad, Jane, that Sharon was killed by a .38 caliber Smith and Wesson close to 9 p.m. Wednesday night. The funeral will be held on Sunday at 2 p.m. in the Presbyterian Church in Vinton. There will not be a wake, and it will be a closed casket."

Neither of us had much more to say, but then the sheriff asked me how dad was taking Sharon's death. I shrugged, because I really didn't know. I had told the sheriff everything I could remember, so I stood up, and he thanked me for coming in. I left his office and the building, pulled out my car keys from my purse, and drove back to the farm. I felt relieved after our conversation. I hoped that what I had told him would lead to the arrest and conviction of the horrible man with the green lizard tattoo and things would get back to normal.

Chapter 11

BY THE TIME dad and Butch finished chores and came inside, I had prepared brunch for us; we didn't eat much. When we finished, Butch and dad went upstairs to shave, shower and dress for the funeral. I knew it was appropriate to wear something dark. I looked through my closet to see what I had hanging in there that was of a "dark" nature. I found a black skirt that I hadn't worn in ages, and a gray and black blouse. I put them on, brushed my teeth, combed my hair and went back downstairs.

It began to rain hard, so we left home a little earlier than we had planned. Dad said he didn't have the exact address of the church, but Vinton is not a large town, so it wouldn't be hard to locate it. Dad took his time driving; the windshield wipers were going back and forth, back and forth. Between the three of us, I don't think we said over twenty words the whole way to Vinton.

We found the stately red-brick church, parked, got out of the car and entered the building. Dad and Butch went to the coatroom to hang up their raincoats and to leave their fedoras. The organist was playing "It Is Not Death to Die." There were a lot of lovely flowers near the altar; the church was almost full. We were ushered to a pew near the back of the church where we sat down. Looking up to the front, we noticed a man, handcuffed, and a policeman walk to a pew near the casket. The man, no doubt, was Sharon's father. He was dressed in a blue suit, white shirt, and striped blue tie.

Then Sharon's family—including the policeman—walked up to the casket and knelt down while the minister quietly prayed with them.

Chapter 12

WE RACED STORMY at Independence the following week. Stormy was in the third race on Tuesday and in the second race on Wednesday. She came in second in both races. She probably would have won the race on Wednesday if Stormy hadn't been spooked when Al Hayes, driving Eden's Dawn, fell off his cart. Stormy was leading but when Al Hayes fell, she broke. An ambulance quickly sped to Mr. Hayes as the spectators stood up and gasped in horror, hoping that he wasn't hurt. He wasn't—just shaken up some. Mr. Hayes got up, and waved at the spectators; everyone clapped and then sat back down to watch the remaining races.

Due to all that has happened, I think dad will spend more time at the farm, besides racing season is almost over unless he takes Stormy to a warmer climate during the up-coming winter months. I think racing reminds him of Sharon a lot more than being at the farm.

We are going to race, however, at the Great Jones County Fair here in Monticello, which will be in August. Butch gets the farm chores done as fast as he can that week, so he can watch dad race, and John Boorman would always help too. I want my time free to spend a lot of time with my friends going on rides, playing games, eating fair food and watching the entertainment. At all times during the five days of the fair, there is something going on.

Sometimes, when dad needs extra help with Stormy he hires one of the boys that hangs around the barn during fair week. The boys like the money, but more than that, they like being around the drivers and their horses.

Chapter 13

IT IS LATE July. Two men, immaculately dressed in navy blue suits and expensive looking ties got out of their black Ford, came up to our porch and knocked. I opened the door. They introduced themselves as they pulled out impressive badges—Detectives. They asked to speak to dad, Butch and me. I noticed their shiny shoes which must be Florsheims; we very seldom see anyone around here dressed so nicely.

I told the detectives that dad and Butch were both in the oats field, but I would try to get their attention by driving our car to the field. They accepted; we got in their car, and drove back to the field. It wasn't long, and Butch noticed us. He drove over to the fence, got off the tractor—letting it run—pulled down the top wires of the fence, so he could get across it, and came over to the car. I introduced them to Butch.

"Hello, Butch," Detective Manley said as he shook Butch's hand. "Sorry to interrupt you. This is Detective Bagetti." They shook hands and then the detectives pulled out their badges.

"We'd like to talk to you and Mr. Ahlrichs about Sharon Hanson's murder. Would it be too much trouble to get Mr. Ahlrichs over here?" Detective Manley asked.

"No trouble. Wait here and I'll go get Tom," Butch said as he managed to get over the fence again, get on the tractor, and look for dad who was driving a tractor pulling the grain wagon.

It wasn't long and dad drove the tractor up to the fence, got off, and turned the motor off; then climbed over the fence like Butch did. It was about their break time, anyway, and I have a fresh warm chocolate cake waiting for them.

The two detectives introduced themselves to dad, and again, pulled out their badges. They told him they had a few questions they wanted to ask about Sharon: what his relationship was to her, did she use drugs, did she have enemies other that who shot her, did he have any other funs than the rifles he had shown the sheriff, etc. They asked me to describe the man

I had seen Sharon with that day in Maquoketa, and to tell them what was said during the argument with that man.

Dad asked the detectives if they had talked to Sharon's ex-husband. They had. He had taken both the kids to Disneyland, in California, the week Sharon was killed. Dad also asked about fingerprints. They said they were working on that. Before the detectives left, Butch and I assured them that dad didn't kill Sharon and that the three of us were home the night she was killed playing cards until midnight.

The detectives didn't stay too long. They put away their notepads, and gave me a ride back to the house, thanked me, and left leaving their card. I wished I had taken my camera to the field and gotten a picture of dad and Butch with the detectives, so that one day I could show my grandkids it. Actually though, I wished that I could expunge all the worry, humiliation and grief this has caused dad. But, it happened, Sharon is dead, and nothing can change that.

Chapter 14

IT WAS THE last week in July, when our neighbor, Mrs. Boorman called to ask me if I would like to ride to Cedar Rapids with her. She was going there to buy her boys new school clothes. I wanted to go. Mom sent me $500.00 to buy school clothes for my senior year. Even though I was just 17, I had been moved up a year in school because mom had spent a lot of time teaching me when I was real young. So I would be 17 when I graduated.

I had made a list of what I wanted to buy including a heavy winter coat for dad that I would give to him on his birthday in November.

It took us about an hour to get to Cedar Rapids. Mrs. Boorman knew a good place to park the car in the area where the best stores were. We must have been in ten shops and bought everything we had gone to Cedar Rapids for. Then we ate lunch at a cafeteria. The food was so appetizing it was hard to decide what to get, but we both decided on roast beef, mashed potatoes, green beans and a roll. And then, there was a delectable banana crème pie!

We loaded up the many packages we had and put them in the trunk of Mrs. Boorman's car feeling exhilarated and worn out. I loved my new clothes and I knew dad would like the jacket. I bought two dresses, three woolen skirts with matching sweaters, two pairs of shoes, bobby socks and panties.

On the way back to Monticello, Mrs. Boorman told me about a terrible experience she had had two years ago. We knew she had been in the hospital, but we didn't know any details. She had gone in the local hospital for a minor surgery, and two days after she was home, she had a panic attack. She told me that she had never heard of anyone having a panic attack, and it seemed the doctors hadn't either. A representative from a mental hospital that the local hospital called in, suggested she check herself into the mental hospital she represented, and believing this was the right thing to do, Mr. Boorman drove her to the mental hospital and she checked herself in. It was a big mistake, but at the time, it seemed like it was the right thing to do. The panic attack, she said, caused her to want to walk around the farm at night, pace the floor, make blubbering sounds and she couldn't concentrate.

As the days passed, it became obvious that Mrs. Boorman was not getting help. The hospital was built to help alcoholics, drug addicts, and severely depressed people. She didn't fit into any of those categories. Not knowing what to say, I just sat and let her talk.

She told me how cruel the staff was to the patients. Men and women were roomed on the same hall which scared her, and she got little sleep because staff members would come into her room day and night to see if anyone was smoking or doing anything they shouldn't be doing. There were no radios, telephones, or television. If anyone did anything out of line, they were sent to E hall where the real "nuts" were. The psychiatrist she saw for a few minutes every day did nothing except keep her drugged and continually changed her drugs. The night before Mrs. Boorman was going to leave the hospital, she had taken her sleeping pill about 9 p.m. At midnight a staff member brought in a roommate. The roommate noticed that the small bathroom was on fire. If the staff member hadn't brought the roommate in at that time, Mrs. Boorman said she probably would have burned to death.

Abruptly, Mrs. Boorman changed the subject and we began talking about our church activities, the farms and our families. After spending the whole day with her, I hoped I would be a lot like her when I became an adult. She is a good Christian woman and quite beautiful. It makes me feel good to know she is over her anxiety problem.

Chapter 15

IT IS AUGUST, hot, and time to combine oats. John Boorman is helping Butch and dad with combining, so that dad and I will have more time to work with Stormy. Butch and John get along famously.

The races in Monticello will be held on the 21st and 22nd of this month. Dad is going to race Stormy on Wednesday the 21st, and he is going to race Kahoka for Jake Miller, on Thursday the 22nd. Jake has gotten too old to race, but he still wants to be a part of the racing circuit. Jake's colors are green and white; dad's are deep purple and white. The races in Monticello are important to us because it is our hometown, and our friends look forward to seeing dad race every summer.

The Fairgrounds is a well manicured city park overlooking a beautiful golf course and the Maquoketa River. The fair actually goes back as far as 1853 as a celebration of the harvest. It was first at Bowen's Prairie, and then Anamosa, but ended up in Monticello, Iowa, in 1874 and has been held there ever since. Records tell us that in 1869, there were stables built there and we know that in 1874, the track was enlarged from a quarter mile to one half a mile.

The five days of the fair is truly the five best days of summer to me. Being there is like walking from reality into a magic kingdom filled with carny music, thrilling rides, tasty fair food, Hollywood entertainment, horse and stock car racing, tractor pulls and games. Many farmers bring their best livestock in to be judged, and their wives bring in their recipe specialties for the same.

Dad knows that I want to spent most of the fair days with my friends, so he hired a guy he saw looking at the horses and petting them. His family had recently moved to town; his dad was a veterinarian. I found out real soon that his name was Mike Collins. He was going to help with both Stormy and Kahoka. Every time I saw Mike, a strange sensation came over me, and I found myself spending mornings of the fair days at the barn to see and talk to him. Mike was taller than me, good looking, and would also be a senior when school started again; however, he would be going to the Catholic School. At the barn, he wore cut-offs, checkered shirts, and tennis shoes. He stayed dirty and sweaty, but to me, he looked like a prince.

Mike and I spent two nights watching the entertainment together eating caramel corn and drinking cokes. He had thought to bring a blanket for us to sit on. We sat on the hillside where we could see the stage and the entertainers perform. Sammy Kay performed one night, and Candy Candido the last night.

Chapter 16

AFTER WATCHING CANDY Candido, we decided to leave the fair. We headed for the main gate. There was the man I had seen pushing Sharon around. He was also leaving the fairgrounds and was walking with a man about forty years old with salt and pepper hair cut short. I told Mike to wait for me at the gate. I followed the men two blocks where they got in a 1949 black Ford and drove away. Back inside the gate, there was a policeman and he called the sheriff for me.

Chapter 17

ON SEPTEMBER 2ND, every student in town found themselves sitting in a desk in a classroom at school. The public school that I attend has three levels; top level is for high school students, the middle level is for the junior high and elementary students, and the bottom level is where the music and home economics rooms are. The large imposing building is red brick with tall shade trees gracing the grounds. Behind the building are tennis courts, the baseball diamond and the play area. The engineers do a great job keeping the building in good shape and clean. We were told in biology class that the floors are granite—a coarse-grained igneous rock used for endurance and steadfastness. These floors have been walked on by many many people for many many years and still look like new. The grounds are well maintained.

Chapter 18

RIGHT AFTER MIKE gave me his class ring, I made a beeline to my four best girlfriends to show them the ring. Faren was first. She was at her locker getting out a book for class when I found her. Faren has long silky blond hair, captivating green eyes, and a figure we all wished we had. Faren said, "Congratulations," with a pretty smile. Katie Mary walked up to us to see what was going on, and I showed her the ring. She giggled. Kaitlen,—Katie Mary—is petite and very trendy; slender with long glossy dark hair, long black eyelashes, and smooth skin. The three of us walked down the hall and found Madison—Maddie—and when she saw the ring, she glowed. Madison is intelligent and beautiful; long brown hair and blue eyes. Kimi I found next. She has short curly auburn hair, green eyes, and, no doubt, will be our class valedictorian. The bell rang, so she glanced at the ring and nodded. Then we raised our hands and did a high five!

For weeks, I adored Mike, but as time passed, I saw a side of him that I didn't like. He became possessive and petulant. He resented the time I spent with my girlfriends and our cheerleading activities. He was often arrogant and didn't make many friends—if any. When we parked to make-out, he pressured me for intimacy which I was not ready for. By November, I was very frustrated with him and planned to give his ring back to him. I still had feelings for him, but I felt he had problems that I couldn't solve. I had wanted to invite Mike to dad's birthday party at which time I presented dad with the warm winter jacket I had bought for him, but I didn't.

About a week after dad's birthday, a friend of mine who is in Mike's class called me one night to let me know that Mike was also going with a girl who attended their school. They would walk hand-in-hand through the halls and he was wearing <u>her</u> class ring around his neck. The girl's name is Sondi Schlegal. That was "the straw that broke the camel's back." From then on, I didn't take his phone calls, nor did I return his ring.

Chapter 19

IN NOVEMBER, THE police had located the man I saw pushing Sharon around. They had taken him into custody and wanted me to identify him in the jail in Anamosa, which I did the next morning. It was the same man, the man with the lizard tattoo on his arm. This was all fine and good, except Jim Kaponi had an airtight alibi. The night Sharon was shot he was in Ron's poolroom in Anamosa from 7:30p.m. 'til the establishment closed at 1 a.m. The detectives had talked with each of the twelve men that were there that night, so Jim Kaponi was free to go. Every man said Jim Kaponi had been in the poolroom from 7:30p.m. 'til 1 a.m. that night.

Hearing the phone ring, Butch picked up the headpiece of our old crank phone that hangs on the wall in the hall.

"Hello," Butch said. He put his mouth close to the speaker.

"Hi dad, it's Gary," Butch's son said.

"It's Gary," Butch whispered to me. I caught his "clue" and left the room so they could talk in private.

After supper, Butch told us that Gary had called to ask if it would be alright with us for him to visit. Butch, I could tell, was real excited about seeing his son again. Dad assured Butch that it would be alright for Gary to come, in fact, he said it would be great having him here.

"I'll put him to work," dad retorted. Butch and I both laughed at his comment.

Gary is in the Air Force and stationed at Offutt Air Force Base in Omaha, Nebraska. He told Butch he would be at the farm on Saturday. It would take him about six hours driving the 300 miles across I-80, and he would be at the farm about 2 p.m.

On Saturday, when the three of us saw Gary's '53 maroon Ford pull up in our driveway, the three of us went out to welcome him. Butch (which I thought was odd) shook hands with Gary instead of hugging him. Butch introduced Gary to us, got Gary's luggage out of the car and carried them inside. When Gary got inside, he said "Something like food smells very good."

"I thought you would be hungry after the long drive, so I prepared dinner. We can eat now if you like," I said. We did. The four of us sat down at the kitchen table, and before we passed the food around, daddy said "Grace." Then we devoured the ham, scalloped potatoes, stewed tomatoes, pear salad, rolls and milk. The meal was topped off with warm rhubarb-strawberry pie and ice cream. The men drank coffee with their pie.

Gary and Butch thanked me for a delicious meal, and then the men left the kitchen and went into the living room to smoke and talk. I cleaned up the kitchen and felt proud that they enjoyed the meal. Later, I showed Gary his room and gave him a tour of the house. After he put his clothes away and put up his toiletries, he went outside to join his father and my dad.

The first minute I laid eyes on Gary, he took my breath away. When he got out of his car, I could tell he was about 6'2" tall with short black hair, fascinating dark brown eyes, and a personality that could charm a bear! I knew this by the look on his handsome face. He was wearing a knee-length black and gray tweed coat with black gloves; he dressed trendy and I liked that. He also had a good build. I wondered if he had a girlfriend. Why not!

Gary went to church with us on Sunday and was introduced to the members of the church including the Boorman brothers, Mark and Jeff. They immediately liked Gary and wanted to know all about life in the Air Force. They said they would come over to the farm during the week. Gary liked the idea. He liked people and would tell the boys and all of us what it is like being in the service.

Gary was eager to help with the chores. He would get up early, and work late. I became fascinated with him and found myself going along with him to help him so I could be near him. Gary and I soon discovered that we felt a love for one another and began going to movies, eating out at night and taking long drives around the countryside. It was so premature, but I knew then that this was the man I wanted to spend the rest of my life with.

The second week Gary was at the farm, dad and Butch drove into Chicago to look at some horses and also farm equipment that was on sale. I stayed home from school those two days to be with Gary. That night for supper I baked a chicken and we had mashed potatoes, gravy, lettuce salad, green beans, rolls and apple pie. After we both cleaned up the kitchen, I found a bottle of wine and we each drank two glasses before going up for bed.

That night we slept in my bed and made tender love and talked about our futures. I laid in his arms until 7 a.m., got up, showered and dressed. Then I went into the kitchen and made bacon and eggs, juice and coffee. I found English Muffins and popped them in the toaster for us.

Gary said he would try to get back to see me on any weekend he could and that I could visit him in Omaha too. He would get back for my Senior Prom and my graduation, and in June, he would be out of the service. Gary had studied insurance and business classes at the University of Nebraska at Omaha and wanted to open an Agency. He said he would be glad to help dad and Butch with the farm and sleep—in his own bed—until he could get the agency open. Gary, before he left, gave me a gorgeous engagement ring and told me to wear it on my right hand so there wouldn't be gossip at school. He also told me that he had something important to tell me—later.

Chapter 20

A FEW DAYS after Gary left for Omaha, Sheriff Wilson stopped by the farm. He had some new information. Mrs. Tobiason, the owner of the building where Sharon had lived upstairs, was painting the apartment. While moving the desk away from the wall so she could paint behind the desk, she found a sheet of paper that somehow the police didn't find. She read it and gave it to Sheriff Wilson. The letter indicated that Sharon had been blackmailing her boss, Karl Helgens, for many months. Evidently, Sharon had gone back into the shop one evening and walked in on Karl and his secretary, Gloria. Neither of them were dressed, and they were embraced on a large couch in Karl's office. Sharon's letter was very explicit about that. Of course, this gave a whole new light on the investigation.

Sheriff Wilson made us promise not to share this information with anyone, because he was not at liberty to discuss the case with anyone except the law.

Karl Helgens was a member of the Lions Club. They had a meeting the night Sharon was killed. "Rumor" was that Sheriff Wilson asked some of the members if Karl had attended the meeting that Wednesday night and what time was the meeting over. The meeting was adjourned at 8 p.m. Sharon was shot about 9 p.m. Karl left when the meeting was over at 8 p.m.

Sheriff Wilson and two of his policemen pulled up to the Helgen's home and rang the doorbell. Mrs. Helgens invited them to come into her living room and asked them to sit down.

"I know you are here about the murder," she quietly said. "I don't feel I can help you. I barely knew Sharon Hanson. She worked for my husband."

"Mrs. Helgens," Sheriff Wilson said. "We're sorry to intrude on your privacy, but, yes, we need to talk to you about the death of Sharon Hanson. First of all, does your husband own a gun?" the sheriff asked.

"Why, yes, he does. I suppose you want to see it," she quietly mumbled. Lauren Helgens was a petite lady with short blond hair. She wore a cross around her neck. She kept their lovely home neat and it was lavishly furnished. Mrs. Helgens was told that they would need to take the gun and the sheriff wrote her out a receipt. The gun was a .38 caliber Smith and Wesson! They asked her if she could remember what time her husband had returned home from the Lions Club meeting that Wednesday night, and she said, "9:30 p.m." Then she began to sob with her head in her hands. The men waited until she had composed herself and then they thanked her and let themselves out the front door.

The lawmen were baffled as to why Karl, if he did kill Sharon, had kept the gun in his home. If ballistics showed that the bullet that killed Sharon came from this gun, Karl would probably go to prison or the electric chair. The men also thought it odd that no one heard the shot that night, however, not many people lived on First Street, or maybe Karl had muffled the sound somehow.

Chapter 21

CHRISTMAS WAS SPENT at the farm with dad and Butch. The Boormans came over after church for dessert. The boys, Jeff and Mark wanted to know when Gary would be back.

Gary called Christmas night and asked me if I would care to drive to Omaha the weekend of New Years. He would get a guest cottage on base. Dad said it was alright with him as long as the weatherman didn't forecast a bad storm.

When Gary's friends, Bill and Bette Suter found out that I was going to be with Gary over New Years, they offered him their mobile home which was parked in a mobile home park close to the base. He cancelled the reservation for the cottage on base. Bill was also in the Air Force.

Dad filled my car up with gas and checked the oil and tires. My ice scraper was in the glove compartment and I had my license and insurance information. While dad did all this, I packed what I thought I would need in Omaha: woolen slacks, sweaters, blouses, socks and panties, jewelry, pajamas, a woolen scarf and mittens and a heavy coat with a hood. My toiletries were in a small bag. I had $200.00 with me.

Gary had given me exact directions as to where the Offutt Mobile Home Park was, and I found it without any problem. The lot number was 62. Gary was there waiting for me with hugs and kisses and then he carried my suitcase and small bag into the mobile home and showed me each room. It was bright, clean and cozy. Then I put away my clothes. Gary had a duffle bag and I didn't ask what he wanted to do with whatever was in it.

Gary went to the refrigerator and got out a Pepsi for each of us. He sat beside me on the couch and told me about his plans for our time together and asked me if they sounded alright. They did.

That night we found a pizza parlor and had the best pizza I had ever tasted along with a salad and Pepsi. We drove around awhile, out by the base, and then back to the mobile home and watched television.

Even though I felt guilty about it, we made love again that night while listening to soft enchanting music on Bill's record player.

The next morning, after pancakes and bacon, I cleaned up the kitchen and made the bed. Gary wanted to take me to the Riverview Zoo in Omaha to see the exotic animals which was fine with me, since in Iowa, we don't have what one would call an exotic animal. Before we left, the phone rang. It was Bill and Bette Suter calling from Denver where they were visiting relatives. They wanted to make sure we were comfortable and had everything we needed; they left their phone number in Denver where they could be reached.

We spent most of the day admiring the thousands of animals, reptiles and butterflies. It was 35 degrees, so we stayed inside the exhibits most of the day.

On the way back to the trailer park, we stopped at a small diner and had burgers, fries, and root beer floats. Gary put change in the jukebox and told me to pick out some good songs. My favorite song was Young Love sung by Sonny James, so I played it first, then Blueberry Hill by Fats Domino, then Love Me Tender by Elvis Presley, I Was the One by Elvis Presley and finally Little Darlin' by the Diamonds. We both loved the popular songs.

"Do you like to dance?" Gary asked me.

"Yes," I said, "But we can't dance here."

"I know," Gary replied, "but I know a great place where we can. It's at 19th and Dodge and called the Music Box. Let's go tonight."

"Ok," I said excitedly.

We left the Music Box about midnight and drove straight back to the trailer park. Gary parked the car, and I started to get out. "Wait," Gary said. "I have something I need to tell you."

Moving closer to him, I put my head on his shoulder. It was snowing now—large white flakes; soon it would look like a fairyland outside.

Gary cleared his throat, and began to stutter as he talked. When his "confession" was over, he looked down at the steering wheel, and then turned to look at me, I suppose to see what my reaction was. I found myself moving away from him. From his "confession" I learned that back in September he had gone back to Washington to attend a funeral. He went out one night with a girl named Crystal, and got her pregnant. I thought how does a funeral and sex coincide? He told me that he didn't love the girl, in fact, he barely knew her, but when later, she told him she was pregnant, he asked her to marry him because he wanted to raise his child. However, the girl wasn't interested in marriage or having a baby for that matter. She told Gary that she was having too much fun to be tied down.

I was furious! I had never been so mad and hurt in my life. The child was conceived before I met Gary, but I couldn't seem to handle this. I felt betrayed. He had even been sending money to the "tramp" as I thought of her, so she could buy baby furniture and baby clothes.

After getting out of the car, I slammed the door. Gary got out and pulled out the trailer keys from his pocket and opened the door. Neither of us said a word for a good while. Then I told Gary that I was going to get my things and go back to Monticello, but he finally convinced me to stay the night because a lot of snow had fallen and the roads would be icy and maybe even closed.

That night, I put on my woolen pajamas, laid on the couch and tried to sleep. In the morning, Gary wanted to fix breakfast for me before I left, but I wasn't interested in food! I told Gary that I needed time away from him. As I gathered my things, he told me he would call me, but I didn't know if I ever wanted to hear from him again. I drove away.

It had stopped snowing and I-80 was clear of ice and snow, but I hardly noticed. There wasn't a lot of traffic either.

My emotions were running wild. Off and on, tears streamed down my cheeks. Both dad and Butch would question me as to why I was home so soon—I could tell dad, but I didn't think it was my place to tell Butch. Gary would have to "drop the bomb" on Butch himself.

That night, Gary called to make sure I had gotten home alright. At first we had small talk going between us. I got the feeling that Gary wanted to believe everything was just fine and dandy. He told me how much he loved me and that he wanted to marry me just as soon as he was out of the service and had a good job.

"I thought you wanted to marry Crystal," I snapped rudely. Gary didn't reply to my remark. He said he would call me the next night.

The next day, I told dad about the trip to Omaha and why I had left there earlier than I had planned to. Dad talked with me for a long while and told me that if Gary and I really loved each other, we should continue the relationship and that I would learn to accept the child, after all, the child would be living in Washington, not Iowa. Would I be able to do that? I didn't know.

After the holidays, I went back to school and spent a lot of time with my girlfriends. Katie Mary was the only friend I confided in about the baby. She hugged me and told me she believed everything would work out.

Chapter 22

GARY CAME TO see me in March and I invited him to my prom and to my graduation. The prom would be in April and the graduation in May. On June 5th, he would be a civilian again. He pressured me to let him know whether he should go back to Seattle, or work on the farm until he found a good job in the insurance field. I wasn't wearing the engagement ring.

Late in March, Gary called and asked me what the color of my prom dress was so he would know what color corsage to buy. I had just bought the dress, and it was truly beautiful; egg-shell white, strapless, knee-length, and the full skirt glittered with rhinestones when the skirt swayed. I planned to wear pearl earrings and a pearl necklace. Mom sent me a bottle of Soir de Paris—I was set for the prom.

There was Faren with Hunter, Katy with Cord, Madison with Stone, and Kimi with Carter. After Gary pinned on the lovely corsage full of peach and white roses, he escorted me to the prom. It was a wonderful evening.

Graduation was on Friday night, May 23rd. We wore gray robes, so it didn't matter what attire we wore underneath them. After we received our diplomas, Gary, and my girlfriends and their dates came out to the farm for refreshments. We were happy. It was 1 a.m. when everyone left, except Gary.

Gary spent the night in our spare bedroom, and left on Sunday. Again, before he left, he told me he needed to know where to go on June 5th. Would it be Stormy Acres, or Seattle?

I loved Gary, but I still wasn't sure if I wanted to marry him now—or ever. Maybe it would be better, I thought, if he went back to Seattle, and in time, maybe I would be able to find the correct answer for us both.

Chapter 23

THE NEXT MORNING, I called Pastor Young, and asked if he would help me with a personal problem that I hadn't been able to solve. At 2 p.m. I was on Highway 38 driving dad's pick up to the church which was only three miles from our farm.

I parked, and as I got out of the car, not bothering to take the keys out or lock the doors, I noticed the side door of the church was open. Pastor Young was standing there holding the door open for me.

"Hello, Jane," Pastor Young enthusiastically greeted me with a man's middle-aged mature voice.

"Come in."

This was the first time I could remember ever seeing Pastor Young wear a suit instead of his long white robe that he wore on Sunday mornings or when he was officiating at other church functions. The burgundy-colored vest he had on under his suit jacket matched the small threads in his suit. He looked nice. He was very tall and slender with salt and pepper hair.

We walked into his office. "Sit down, Jane. I'm glad to see you. How can I be of help to you?" he asked as he offered me some red licorice which I accepted. I hurriedly began to blurt out the whole story from the day I first met Gary. Pastor Young asked me to slow down, so he could keep up with my story. We both laughed; I began to relax while he listened intently. He counseled me for about an hour; we read Bible verses and he explained what they meant and how they applied to my situation. He talked about Gary's sin and reminded me that <u>we all</u> sin. He said that God is pleased that Gary wants to be a part of his child's life, and that He would be proud of me if I would be too.

Before long, I felt God's love come into my heart.

Before I left Pastor Young's office, we said the Lord's Prayer. I thanked him and drove back to the farm with a whole new perspective and a better attitude. My mind was clear now, and the world was much brighter. I could hardly wait to get home to call Gary. Soon, I would be a bride.

Chapter 24

GARY SAID HE would be in Monticello late in the day on June 5th. He called his grandparents in Seattle to let them know that he was going to the farm and he made sure they wrote down the telephone number and address while they talked. Gary assumed they already had both since Butch had lived at the farm for a long time, but he wanted to make sure. Butch had their telephone number and address too. Gary asked his grandmother if they had heard anything from Crystal, but they hadn't.

About noon on June 5th, Gary loaded his car up with his clothing, camera, sports equipment and other paraphernalia he had accumulated while in the military. He had already said goodbye to his buddies and had given Bill Suter the telephone number and address of the farm, so they could keep in touch. Gary had asked Bill to be his best man at the wedding, and Bill said he would be honored. As he drove out of the base, the air policeman at the gate waved him out.

A few miles from the base, Gary stopped at the Sinclair gas station. The investigators couldn't determine if he had stopped for gas, to have the air checked in his tires, or to buy snacks or something to drink because by the time the police arrived at the station not one of the three people in the station were alive.

Chapter 25

THE TELEPHONE RANG about 3 p.m. Butch had just come into the house for a drink and something to eat. It had been real hot outside all week and he was enjoying being inside where it was cooler, and almost didn't answer the phone.

"Hello," Butch said holding his glass of iced tea.

"Is this Butch Benson, the father of Gary Benson?"

"Yes, I'm his dad," Butch answered.

"Mr. Benson, I'm Detective Ed Egger. I work the Sarpy County area, and especially Bellevue. I hate giving you bad news over the phone, and I apologize."

"Is my son in jail or hurt?" Butch inquired.

"Mr. Benson, Gary was shot earlier today when he stopped at a Sinclair Gas Station not far from the base. The place was being robbed and Gary just happened to be there at the wrong time. The police called his grandparents (the Hamiltons) and they have requested that his body be flown to Seattle. Do you have their telephone number and address?"

"Yes, of course. I will call them now to see about arrangements."

"Oh, one more thing Mr. Benson, Bill Suter, a friend of Gary's is driving Gary's car to Monticello tomorrow. I hope that is alright with you."

"Yes, that is awfully nice of Mr. Suter."

"Again, Mr. Benson, I am sorry to give you the news by telephone, and my deepest sympathies to you," the detective said kindly.

Butch thanked the detective for calling, and then hung up the phone.

Twisting my diamond ring-which was back on my left hand, the sun made it shine like a brilliant star. It was June 5th and my head was in the clouds. I was almost skipping as I walked into the kitchen after helping dad with some chores when I noticed Butch sitting at the table with his head in his hands. My first thought was that he was sick, so I asked him if I should get dad.

Chapter 26

"JANE," BUTCH SAID very softly. I could hardly hear him. "Sit down honey. I don't want to tell you this, in fact, I don't know how to tell you this, but just believe that somehow we will get through it."

Butch was ill, that was it. He was sick but he would get well. That's all it was I tried to convince myself. The next thing I remember was Butch lifting me up from the floor and laying me on the sofa. He went to the sink and got a wet towel and put it on my forehead and then he ran outside to get dad. Dad told me that Gary was dead.

When I opened my eyes, Mrs. Boorman, I noticed, was sitting in a rocking chair close to my bed. The room was quiet except for the soft soothing sound of the runners on the rocker as they slowly moved in rhythm. Mrs. Boorman was praying softly in German with her head down. It was dark with only shadows moving around the room which the branches on the tall maple trees were sharing with us. It was raining and there were far away sounds of thunder as if someone was playing a timpani. The darkness, the pitter-patter of the rain, along with the low grunts of thunder lulled me into a semi-conscious sleep.

The small clock in my bedroom said 9 a.m. I could hear Mrs. Boorman moving around in the kitchen downstairs. Obviously, she was making breakfast because I could smell bacon. I got out of bed, put on my robe, tightened the sash and walked slowly down the stairs.

"You stayed all night with me, didn't you Mrs. Boorman?" I asked.

"Yes honey," she answered ruefully. "I'll stay as long as you want me to," she assured me.

"Can you eat something or at least drink some juice?" Mrs. Boorman asked.

"No, thank you. I don't care for anything right now," I replied. I sat down at the kitchen table and watched Mrs. Boorman as she worked. I wondered where dad and Butch were, but I was groggy and didn't feel like conversation.

"Jane," Mrs. Boorman began. "Butch is going to Seattle for the funeral. He talked to the Hamiltons last night; they are making the funeral arrangements, and told Butch about a nice motel close to their home. They asked if you were going too."

"If Butch is going, then I want to go too," I said. "Mrs. Boorman," I asked, "Do you think I should call my mother?"

"I meant to tell you Jane," she said. "Your dad called your mother after you fell asleep last night and told her about Gary. She didn't want your dad to wake you, but to tell you that she is sorrowful and will call you soon."

I missed talking to mom, but I didn't know if I wanted to visit her. She has been engaged to a rich man who has tobacco shops all over the U.S., Europe, and Canada. I resent him because I believe he is the reason that mom left us. Maybe, I thought, there'll come a day I'll be able to accept her leaving, but my pain was still too deep.

Chapter 27

CLOSE TO 2 p.m. on June 6th, Bill Suter drove up our lane driving Gary's car followed by another car. Mrs. Boorman opened the door to let them in. They were in civilian clothes and each was carrying something. Mr. Suter - Bill - introduced himself, and the other man to Mrs. Boorman and then Bill walked over to me and took my hands with tears in his eyes. I looked up into his eyes, took my hands away from his, and put my arms around him. We were both hurting. The man who drove the second car was another friend of Gary's. His name was Lance Lawson.

Bill had brought me beautiful red roses tied with a white and red lace bow and Lance handed me a large box of candy, best of all, they gave me a large picture of the three of them: Gary, Bill and Lance, all in uniform. How thoughtful I thought fighting back tears.

Mrs. Boorman went outside to get Butch and dad. In a few minutes, they came in and shook hands with the men. We all talked for about thirty minutes and invited the men to spend the night, but they had made arrangements with Bill's sister who lives in Anamosa. He was anxious to see his niece and nephew. I told them that Butch and I were going to Washington. Before they left the house, I kissed them both.

Then Butch made all the reservations for the two of us. We would fly out of the Cedar Rapids Municipal Airport the next day and get a rental car at the Seattle-Tacoma Airport.

That evening, I called my four best friends to let them know about Gary and my trip to Seattle. All four were in disbelief as I was. They said they would be out to see me when I got back and that made me feel good.

John, Mrs. Boorman's husband, told dad that he and his boys would do Butch's work in his absence. You couldn't ask for better neighbors.

Chapter 28

IT WAS EARLY evening on the 7th when we pulled into the parking area at the motel the Hamilton's had recommended. Butch got out of the car, went into the office to pay and get our keys. Butch carried the navy blue Samsonite luggage Mrs. Boorman had given me to use on the trip, and then he carried his luggage to his room.

Just a few blocks up the street was a cozy little diner. We ate supper there. Neither of us had much of an appetite. Butch had a cheeseburger, fries and coffee. I had a fish sandwich and a malt. Butch used the payphone to call the Hamiltons to let them know we had arrived in Seattle. They said they would meet us at the church for the visitation the next day at 2 p.m. and asked us if we would follow them to their house where we could talk. Butch agreed.

After a hot shower, I cuddled up to a pillow on my bed. I turned on the television, but couldn't concentrate on whatever movie was on. My thoughts went back to when Sharon died and how devastating it must have been for dad and how hard going to her funeral must have been. Tomorrow would be the last time I would look at Gary. I wasn't looking forward to the next two days.

I thought about Crystal and Gary's baby, and I remembered what Pastor Young had said about how proud God would be if I would be a part of the child's life. That seemed impossible now. I wasn't even sure if Crystal would be at the funeral, but if she was, I wanted to meet her, I knew that.

Chapter 29

THE CHURCH OF Christ was located on 8th Avenue and West Halladay on Queen Anne Hill. The church was old, and had a lot of character. It looked serene, and as if time hadn't played games with it.

Butch parked the rental car in the parking lot; we got out and walked to the wide front doors where we could already hear soft music. I became afraid and didn't want to go in, but before I could think about that any further, the Hamilton's came up to greet us. I could tell they were happy we were there. Mr. Hamilton showed Butch where he could leave his fedora, and Mrs. Hamilton took my arm, and began introducing me to her friends and some of Gary's also. Everyone was nice, genuinely friendly to me. There were a lot of tears, and soon to be more in the sanctuary.

"Do you want to see Gary?" Mrs. Hamilton asked me.

"Yes, I think so. It'll be the last time I will ever see him," I whispered.

She led me over to a small room where there were more flowers than I had ever seen at one time. We walked over to Gary, and stood there, hand-in-hand for a long time. "I love you, Gary—I always will, and I'll love your child too." I promised him.

Mrs. Hamilton and I went back to the sanctuary, and sat down by her husband and Butch. When the service was over, everyone slowly and quietly left. Butch found his fedora, and told me that the Hamiltons had invited us to their home so we could talk in private. We followed them in our rental car.

We had just stepped out of the front doors when I noticed a young pregnant girl coming up the brick stairs. She was with a guy about her age. She was wearing a black and white maternity top with black slacks, and looked as if she was about seven months along. Our eyes met; I think my heart skipped a beat. I wasn't prepared for this.

"Are you Crystal Emerson?" I asked. "I'm Jane Ahlrichs, Gary's fiancée." Then my mind went blank.

"Yes, I'm Crystal; this is my boyfriend Buzz," she said.

I wished Buzz would "buzz off." He looked awful. He was chubby, if not fat, his clothes looked as if he had slept in them, and I wondered how long it had been since he had had a haircut.

"Hi, Buzz," I said politely. He smelled like stale beer!

"Crystal," I timidly said. "I'd like to talk with you before I go back to Iowa. Could we meet tomorrow after the funeral?"

"Where?" she asked.

"How about your parents' house?" I asked.

"I've been staying with Buzz, but that will be alright. Buzz is looking for a job, so he won't be with me," she said.

I thought, My God, he doesn't even have a job! Crystal reached in her purse and got out a pencil and a small piece of paper and wrote down her parents' address and telephone number. Then she said that Buzz's number had been disconnected. Why would that surprise me? I thought to myself.

"Thank you. I'll see you tomorrow at your parents' home right after the funeral." Then I saw Crystal and Buzz—very late—walk into the church.

Butch had stepped back, but came forward and we walked to the rental car.

Chapter 30

WE FOLLOWED THE Hamiltons to their house designed in a colonial architectural style with stately white columns—two stories and inviting. There was a well manicured hedge around the property on all four sides and many ornamental plants including eucalyptus trees in the front yard. They had nice flowers on them and gave off a nice fragrance.

Mrs. Hamilton opened the door for us and asked us to sit down. Mr. Hamilton offered Butch a drink, which he accepted, and Mrs. Hamilton and I drank tea and then she showed me all the rooms in their home. It was lovely and very different than our home at Stormy Acres.

We walked up the winding stairway and she showed me all the rooms upstairs including the room Gary slept in. I thought it looked typical of a young man's room. There was a desk with a typewriter on it, a lamp, and an assortment of pens and pencils as if they were waiting for someone to pick them up and use them. Gary had put up posters of famous athletes and rock stars on the walls. I noticed a football and a basketball in one of the corners. Mrs. Hamilton asked me if there was anything I would like to keep me from the room, but I declined as not to disturb anything, besides Gary's car was at the farm loaded with his belongings and when I got back to Iowa, I would go through them. There were probably some things the Boorman boys would like to have. Actually, it should be Butch to go through Gary's things.

When we went downstairs and went into the living room where Mr. Hamilton and Butch were, the subject of Crystal came up. Gary had confided in them about the situation. They felt like we should know about Crystal and her past, so there would be no surprises later on. They assured us they were not interested in gossip, but they were concerned about the baby.

"Somewhere along the line," Mrs. Hamilton sighed, "Crystal got off on the wrong road; she dropped out of school, and began smoking and running around with undesirable so-called friends. She, no doubt, is an alcoholic, and word is, she has experimented with drugs. She has had a number of run-ins with the police, and has spent time in the local jail for petty theft; not to mention drinking while driving. She is not the kind of person you can trust. You know,—I didn't know—that she was adopted."

From what we understand, she lives with her mother and stepfather in a large mobile home park. Shirley, Crystal's mother, either owns or works in a supper club, and the father—stepfather—has something to do with a large construction company. Shirley and Don are members of the Catholic Church about a mile from us, and when Don is in town, they both sing in the choir. Shirley also teaches a Confraternities of Christian Doctrine class. I know this because my sister is a member of the same church.

"Please," Mrs. Hamilton said, "I do not mean to be gossiping; I just want you to be aware of what has been going on with Crystal as we are concerned about Gary's child. We know Gary sent Crystal money for a crib and a changing table, and also money for diapers and clothes. We are more than willing to help financially also, but only for the baby, not Crystal!"

I told Mrs. Hamilton that I was going to talk to Crystal the next day after the funeral at the Emersons and that I would get back to her on what I could find out.

"It sure doesn't sound like Crystal will make a good mother." I'm sure I grimaced as I said that. After an hour or so, we got up to leave and thanked them for the drinks.

Butch drove us back to the motel. I asked him if the woman in the large picture hanging on the wall in the Hamilton's living room was his late wife, Sara. The woman in the picture was wearing a gorgeous emerald green gown and pearls. She had been very beautiful if it was Sara, and Butch said it was. He said nothing more about the picture or Sara.

Being busy had somewhat kept my mind off my grief and unhappiness, but sleep didn't come easy that night.

When the service for Gary was over, the casket bearers carried him to the church cemetery where roses were placed on his casket as the speaker from the Church of Christ said a special prayer. As he was lowered into the vault, I felt the earth move under my feet. Butch put his arm around me to hold me as I sobbed. He was crying too. Gary had been his only child.

Chapter 31

CRYSTAL MET US on time at her parents' mobile home like she said she would. Butch didn't want to talk with her, so he stayed in the car.

"Hi Crystal, thank you for coming," I said to myself!

She drove up in a 1949 white Ford. I wondered if she had a license, but I wasn't going into a conversation about her driving record. I didn't want her mad at me, so I was careful not to offend her.

Her stringy long blond hair was loosely hanging down over her shoulders, and she had a lot of make-up on. The maternity dress she wore was quite attractive being black and white. She was wearing what looked like comfortable black flats.

"Hi Crystal," I said as she got out of the Ford. "You look very nice."

"Thanks," she replied. "Why don't we sit outside on the lawn chairs in the shade?" She pulled up one of the chairs for me and said she was going inside and get us something to drink. I made myself comfortable.

When she came out, she had a beer for her and lemonade for me. It was sweet and refreshing. I asked her how she had been feeling and she told me that she still got nauseated sometimes in the mornings, but it hadn't slowed her down any and she laughed loudly. I so wanted to mention that she should not be drinking alcohol or smoking while carrying a baby, but I knew better and I kept my mouth shut. I wanted to be on her good side because of the baby.

Although Crystal certainly was "rough around the edges," the more we talked, the more compassion I felt for her. She was so child-like in ways. She told me she didn't want the baby because she didn't want to have to stay home to take care of the child and besides, she really didn't know what to do for a baby. I asked her when she was due, and she knew exactly, because she was having a Caesarean June 25th at Swedish Medical.

The baby was kicking she said, and asked if I wanted to feel her stomach to feel the kicks. I did and I could feel the baby kicking. How amazing I thought.

"Does it hurt?" I asked her.

"No, it just feels strange," she said.

Thinking that Crystal might decide to give the baby up for adoption, I felt a terrible feeling of anxiety come over me. The baby was becoming real to me—a tiny human that would need nourishment and love.

"Crystal, what would you think about my coming to Seattle after you have your baby to help you for a while? With Gary gone, I don't know what to do with my life yet, and I know I would be a big help to you," I said.

"Sounds like a good idea to me," Crystal replied. "We have four bedrooms. One is small and I have put the crib in it. Wait a minute, she said. "Let me go call my mother."

In a flash, Crystal was back outside with a happy look on her face. She had reached her mother at work and told her what I had suggested. Her mother said she would drive to the motel after work and talk about it. I gave Crystal the name of the motel and my room number. I wondered what Dad and Butch would think about this, but it was something I really wanted to do. I wasn't sure if it was for Gary or for me.

Chapter 32

WHEN I GOT back in the rental car, I apologized to Butch for being so long, but he was alright. He had been listening to something on the car radio. I told him that Mrs. Emerson was coming to my room after she got off work, but I wasn't ready to tell him why.

We ate pizza and salad that night at an Italian restaurant about five miles from the motel. Butch had been so quiet the last few days, but that night, he talked a lot. Maybe it had something to do with the bottle of California Chardonnay he ordered and enjoyed. He was like an uncle to me, and I am sure dad felt like he was a brother to him.

The waiter showed us a piece of heavenly cheesecake, and Cannoli, Italian pastry for dessert, but we had to refuse. We were both "stuffed." Butch paid the bill, tipped the waiter, and we left the restaurant. Then we got in the rental car and headed back to the motel where I would meet Crystal's mother.

Chapter 33

WHEN I GOT back to my room, I hurriedly took a shower, washed and dried my hair; combed it out so it would look good. Then I put on the skirt and blouse I had worn to the restaurant. I so wanted to make a good impression on Mrs. Emerson. I heard a knock at the door, rushed over to turn the television off, and went to the door. Mrs. Emerson had a nice smile on her face as I greeted her, invited her in, and motioned for her to sit down on one of the two chairs I had in the room. I had gotten a few bottles of Pepsi from the machine out in front of the motel, and offered her one, but she wasn't thirsty, but appreciated the offer.

Mrs. Emerson was a petite lady and pretty. She was wearing a green skirt, a green and white striped blouse and white casual looking shoes. She had her hair pulled back in a ponytail with a green ribbon.

As our conversation began and continued, it was very apparent that Shirley—she had asked me to call her Shirley—and Don, her husband, wanted me to return to Seattle when the baby would arrive. She told me all about their mobile home; that it is clean and cozy. They would pay for my airline ticket, and I would have a car to drive. Then she went on to say that they would pay me a weekly allowance. By then, I knew she was very serious.

It was summer, and their jobs were demanding. Shirley mentioned that Crystal's grandmother might come to live with them to take care of the baby, but they needed someone much sooner that she could come—if she did come.

Shirley then brought up the subject of Crystal and her hair-raising past. I think she wanted me to know what I would be up against. She told me that she and Don had brought Crystal up in the Catholic faith, but even Father McCleary hadn't been able to help her. They almost had Crystal put in an institution at one time due to her drug use and alcoholic intake, but the administrators told us up front that if she didn't want help, we would be wasting our money and fooling ourselves that she might change.

Shirley told me that Crystal had been picked up numerous times for shoplifting—items that she had. She had been picked up for driving without a license, DUI, and one time waving a gun around. She lies and does whatever she can get away with.

"Knowing all of that, I'd still like to help" I said ruefully.

We exchanged telephone numbers and addresses and promised to remember the time change when we called. I told Shirley I would call her each week. I walked Shirley to her car and waved as she drove off. Then I got into my silk pajamas, fluffed up a pillow and turned the television back on before I fell asleep. Our flight was to leave tomorrow about 10 a.m., so I would have time to pack and dress in the morning. I would get up about 8 a.m. so we could get some breakfast before going to the airport.

What would Gary think of all this I thought to myself. Neither one of us could have ever imagined things turning out this way. I would be glad to see dad and my dog, Pup, tomorrow and when I found my nerve, I would talk to dad about going back to Seattle. I also needed to decide whether I wanted to go to college or get a job. Or, I wondered, did dad want me to stay and work on the farm.

Chapter 34

IT FELT GOOD to be back home with the smell of newly cut hay that filled the air. For some reason, the aroma seemed to be more profound in the early evening. I loved the farm, but I felt imbalanced and I didn't have the confidence in myself that I had always prided myself with. Everything was the same, but somehow different now.

On the countertops in the kitchen, were two vases of lovely spring flowers, a triple layer chocolate cake, homemade breads and cookies. As dad walked across the room nearing the countertops, he looked at me askance and asked if I had noticed the smoked ham. All of this had come from the Ladies Aid Society at church, and there would be more as this is what the women did when a church family had an illness or a death.

By now, I assumed everyone in town knew about our loss.

The Boormans ate supper with us that night. Mrs. Boorman had baked a large beef roast with a mixture of vegetables, boiled potatoes, rolls and a rhubarb pie. The seven of us sat down and we thanked God for the food and all our blessings. Then I got up to make a pot of coffee so it would be ready when it was time for the pie.

"Dad, where is Gary's car?" I asked.

"I parked it behind the house in the shade. I didn't want the first thing you saw when you got home was Gary's car" he answered.

"I just wondered," I said.

Butch spoke up. "Tomorrow I will go through Gary's things. Jeff and Mark might want some of the sporting equipment and the clothes."

After Mrs. Boorman and I cleared off the table, washed and dried the dishes, the Boormans got up to leave. We thanked them for the wonderful meal and then I gave Mrs. Boorman most of the cookies, bread and chocolate cake for them to take home.

Butch shook hands with John and thanked him for helping dad while we were in Seattle. John said he was happy to help any time.

I told Mrs. Boorman that I would get her suitcases back to her; I hoped she would let me borrow them again when I went back to Seattle.

Chapter 35

AFTER THEY LEFT, dad told me I had a letter and it was on the hutch. I walked over, picked it up and opened it.

"It's from mom," I exclaimed, "and it's postmarked New York. There's a check for $5000," I said incredulously. Dad and Butch didn't say a word. I guess they were too overwhelmed. I read the letter out loud.

> "Dearest Jane,
>
> First of all, I miss you very much, and I wish I could be with you during this sad time. I think of you every day. Jacques and I were married yesterday here in New York in a small chapel, so now my last name is Chirac. By now you have figured out he is French. Please write down the address on the envelope, and I will call you when we get our new telephone number. We have just moved into a lovely apartment and won't get the new number until tomorrow or the day after.
>
> We would love for you to travel to Europe with us on our next trip there.
>
> Please use the check for whatever makes you happy.
>
> Love,
> Mom"

Dad never said why he didn't want me going back to Seattle; however, he didn't tell me not to go. I was glad that I had the $5000 so I could use my own money, and not have to ask dad for any. Dad, I was sure, was still hurting from the loss of Sharon, and he could relate to what I was going through, so maybe that is why he didn't work hard on my not going.

Chapter 36

MY GIRLFRIENDS AND I spent an afternoon together that week. Faren picked me up at the farm; she had her dad's Fairlane. Then the two of us picked up Kim, Katy and Madison.

At first the conversation was low-key, but then when the girls realized I was alright, they began honking at friends we saw in town. They would wave back. We began to tell jokes and laugh about funny things that had happened to us through the years—especially at school. We pulled into an A & W Root Beer stand and ordered sodas. When the girls noticed a car full of "guys" right next to the Fairlane, they began flirting with them, but we didn't want to get involved with any of them—not today, anyway,—so we enjoyed the sodas, waved good-bye and drove off.

When we got back to the farm, I told the girls that I was going back to Seattle to help Crystal with the baby. They were surprised, and didn't like the idea at all. I told them that I wouldn't be there but a week or two, but then I began to wonder if my going was a good idea or not. Maybe I should forget the whole thing and move on with my life. My friends were having fun and I should be too.

More food came from the Ladies Aid Society. I was glad too because I didn't have to spend a lot of time in the kitchen. Talking with Shirley on the telephone wasn't as awkward as I thought it would be. She was kind and considerate I thought. She insisted that she and Don would pay for my ticket; plus I would have a car to use while in Seattle as her brother and his family would be in Florida for the summer and they were planning on leaving the car with Don and Shirley with less chance of it getting stolen. Crystal was not to drive the car at any time.

Shirley told me that Crystal would be having the Caesarean at Swedish Medical Center, which she said, was located on Tallman Avenue, not too far from their mobile home. The Caesarean was still scheduled for June 25th.

Again, Shirley warned me about Crystal; not to expect much of anything from her. They hadn't seen much of her since Butch and I were there. Obviously, Crystal needed a lot of psychiatric help. I began to wonder if I should fear for my life being around her; I also wondered how she would react when the baby arrived. I could just about imagine!

Chapter 37

WHEN MY PLANE landed in Seattle on June 24th, Don and Shirley were both there to meet me. They seemed happy to see me. After we said our "hellos" the three of us walked to the baggage claim and retrieved my suitcases—or rather Mrs. Boormans' suitcases. Then we walked to their car where Don opened the door for me.

During the ride on the streets of Seattle, I learned quite a lot about the Emersons. Don owned half of a large well-known construction company based in Seattle. His company worked in other cities as well. He had come back home to be with Shirley and Crystal during this stressful time. Shirley inherited a supper club—which also served lunches—and she must have really enjoyed it because she talked a lot about her club.

As we pulled up into their front yard, I noticed a small "For Rent" sign on the outside of their picket fence. I was curious about why it was there, but decided to ask about it later.

We got out of the car. Don carried the suitcases and unlocked the trailer door for us. The three of us went inside, and Mr. Emerson put the suitcases in a bedroom for me. Mr. Emerson then asked me to call him Don, which was fine with me. They both treated me like a grown up and I liked that. I felt at ease with them.

Shirley asked us if we were hungry or if we wanted anything to drink, but we both declined her offer. I had eaten on the plane. Then Shirley walked me through the mobile home, pointing out my bedroom, and showing me how to work the thermostat, use the washer and dryer, how to use the garbage disposal, stove, etc. Then she handed me the key to the doors.

My room had a double bed in it with a pretty cherry pattern on the quilt and on the dust-ruffle. The curtains were frilly with the little red cherries on them also. There was a large chest and a dresser with a large mirror. By the bed, a night table with a lamp and a radio on it. I would be the only one that would use the bathroom that was close to my bedroom; however, I thought that it should be shared with Crystal.

Don said that he would like for the three of us to get in the black Buick Roadmaster that I would be using and have me drive it and become comfortable with it and to become familiar with the lights, brakes, etc. Don had drawn out a map that was easy to read showing the names and numbers of the roads and places I would probably want or need to drive to.

"You do have a driver's license, don't you?" Don laughed, but with a serious tone.

"Yes, I do," I said with a soft chuckle. We drove around for about an hour or so passing the hospital, the doctor's office, two malls, a grocery store, and a drugstore. On Don's map too he had written in where a movie theatre was and the location of an opera house. I put the map in the glove compartment so I wouldn't misplace it.

The last establishment we saw was the Rainbow Inn. Don told me to pull in the parking lot, and that we were going to eat there. Sheepishly, I asked if I should call Crystal to join us. Shirley said that she had tried to call Crystal all day, but couldn't reach her. I certainly hoped she would be at the mobile home for us to drive her to the hospital the next day.

By the expressions on the employee's faces, I could see that they liked Shirley, their boss—and liked her a lot. As soon as Don opened the door for us, a waiter greeted us and led us to a table overlooking the water. The tables had linen table cloths on them and linen napkins with nice silverware. The waiter handed us menus, and Don ordered wine and dinner for us.

Before our salmon dinners were brought to our table, a waiter lit the candles on our table. A pianist was playing dreamy music. Oh, what a romantic restaurant this was I thought to myself. Shirley had a good thing going; the customers kept coming in the whole time we were there. The dinner was fabulous. Of course, there was no charge, but Don left the waiter a stupendous tip. I knew I would never forget this night.

Don drove us back to the mobile home park, and it was during this time that I asked about the "For Rent" sign.

"We are having a home built on a golf course; we have been planning this for about two years. Don is an avid golfer. We had hoped that Crystal would either move with us or move in the trailer and raise her baby there. We told her we would give her title to it and even pay the lot rent and utilities; you know, help her out in any way until she can get on her feet, but she has no interest in doing either," Shirley said.

"Damn," Don said. "She doesn't have interest in anything but . . ."

He stopped himself from saying something that we already knew. He was getting mad.

"Maybe in time—after the baby arrives—Crystal will come around and straighten up," Shirley said. "Possibly my sister will come to Seattle or my mother. We need to make definite plans and soon."

Chapter 38

IT WAS WEDNESDAY, June 25, 1958. The pale blue sky was crowded with big white fluffy clouds. Birds were talking to each other, and bushy-tailed squirrels were chasing each other up the trees. It was the type of day I would normally put on my swimming suit, go outside and lay on a lounge chair with a tall glass of lemonade and my radio beside me. Not today though. Today would be a perfect day to be born. What name had Crystal chosen for the baby? I wondered—my mind kept passing from subject to subject.

Crystal was on time. Don and Shirley got up out of their chairs and went out to her car. I saw Crystal get out—she had a small bag with her. They began to get into Don's truck when Shirley turned around and yelled to me that they would call me from the hospital. I nodded.

Chapter 39

IT WAS ABOUT 4p.m. when the phone rang. I ran to pick it up.
"Hello, Jane. It's Shirley. We have a boy!"
"Great" I replied. "How is Crystal?"
"She's fine—sleeping now. The baby is such a little thing; so cute, and very alert already. He weighs 6lbs. and 3 ounces." Shirley happily shared her joy. "Crystal would like to see you."
"Has she named him?" I asked.
"No, she said she wanted to think about it," Shirley said.
"I'll call the hospital tomorrow, and find out when visiting hours are and go up tomorrow afternoon." I said.
"Jane, make yourself at home. There are a lot of books and magazines and there should be some good movies on television and plenty of food in the fridge. We'll see you later."
We said goodbye and hung up. I fixed a sandwich and had a Pepsi, bathed, washed my hair and was asleep before Don and Shirley got home.
The next morning, Shirley went to work and Don headed for the golf course. Don looked just like a typical golfer with his beige-colored slacks, expensive golf shirt, golf shoes and tam that fit perfectly on his head. After the golf game, he was going back to work in Yakima, Washington.
At noon I was able to reach Butch and Dad to tell them about the baby. Butch didn't have much to say. I told dad to put Pup up to the phone to see if he would bark or pant on the phone. I missed my dog. Dad wanted to know when I would get back home. I told him I hoped it would be soon.

Chapter 40

VISITING HOURS BEGAN at 2 p.m. Not wanting to visit Crystal empty-handed, I drove to the first of the two malls Don had drawn on the map, and looked for a lingerie shop. There it was, next to Sears. I parked the car and walked into the shop and began to look around for something that I thought Crystal would like. A clerk came over and offered to help. I ended up buying a lovely light-blue robe, gown and matching slippers that any woman would love. The clerk mentioned they had panties on sale, so I told her to add three pairs to my gifts and to wrap them, which she did in blue and white paper.

I paid the clerk, got back into the car now in the shopping mood, and drove to a large drugstore I had driven by on the way to the mall to get a diaper pail. I was certain I hadn't seen one in the trailer. There was one left on a bottom shelf in the store, so I put it in my cart. Now in the mood to shop, I walked up and down the aisles putting items in my cart that I knew babies needed like baby powder and oil, diaper pins, a brush and comb set, small bars of soap, a thermometer, a plastic bathtub and some salve if the baby got a diaper rash. Evidently a mother instinct that I didn't know was in me came out, because I had never been around a new born before.

If we needed anything else, I would go get it, and hoped there would be other items because I enjoyed driving the car and shopping in stores I had never been in before.

By 2:30 p.m. I had parked the car in the hospital parking area. Taking the packages the clerk had wrapped, I got out of the car making sure to lock the doors so no one would be tempted to steal the other items I had purchased.

My heart was pounding as I rode the elevator up to the maternity floor. The only other "passenger" was a young man carrying a large bouquet of flowers. Lightly I knocked on the door to Crystal's room, but heard nothing; gingerly, I opened the door and peeked in. Crystal was laying back on a pillow looking at a magazine.

"Hi Crystal, may I come in?" I asked.

"Sure" she said.

"How are you?" I asked her.

"Sore as hell, but I want to get out of here as soon as possible," she snapped.

Walking up to her bed, I handed her the gifts; she didn't reach out for them or make any comment so I set them on the window sill and told her that I thought she would like what was in the packages. She still didn't say anything.

"Is there anything I can get for you?" I asked.

"A pepperoni pizza and a beer. Would you get them for me?" she asked.

"Crystal," I said. "I don't know what your doctor wants you to have or not to have, but I'll see what I can do. I am planning on coming back tomorrow. Have you decided on a name for your baby?" I asked changing the subject.

"What do you think I should name him?" she asked.

"Of course, I would like you to name him Gary after his dad."

"Okay," she said. Gary will be his name and Harrison will be his middle name."

"I like that. Is Harrison a name that is in your family or the name of a friend?" I asked.

Crystal chuckled. "In a class in school we learned about our ninth president whose last name was Harrison. The reason I remember it so well is that he was only president for 32 days because he got sick. I just liked the name. Sad to become president and die after 32 days."

Not wanting to get into a discussion about Crystal's education at this point and time, I asked her where the babies were. She told me that they were down the hall to the right of her room. I excused myself and left her room. It is hard to find the words to explain how I felt at that time. I wanted to see baby Gary, and at the same time, I didn't want to see him; I was afraid of what my feelings would be. In less than a minute, I found out.

There he was in his little oblong bassinet sound asleep with two fingers touching his cheek. His bassinet was the only one that didn't have a nametag on it. There was a blue cap on his head and nothing else except a diaper.

Hot tears began rolling down my cheeks. I felt what I thought might be anxiety like Mrs. Boorman had suffered with; it's a feeling very hard to explain. Afraid that I would start wailing, I walked farther down the hall and found a ladies' room. I stayed in there until I could calm myself down and not make a spectacle of myself in front of anyone.

Then, not saying goodbye to Crystal, I got out of the building and got into my car breathing heavily, and drove back to the trailer. I was terribly emotional.

Later that day I called the Hamiltons to tell them that Crystal now had a baby boy. They wanted to know if I would stop by their home before I left Seattle because Mrs. Hamilton had shopped for the baby, things, she said, like sheets, blankets and some pajamas that he would grow into. I told them that I would see them before I left.

Chapter 41

IT STARTED TO thunder. I made sure all the windows were closed so if it rained hard, nothing would get wet. Then I went out to do the same with the windows in Crystal's car. Before I was getting out of the back seat, I noticed something under the front passenger's seat. Being the curious creature that I am, I pulled it out from under the seat. It was a dark green metal box that had a small unlocked latch. It was raining hard now, but I had shut the car windows so nothing would get wet. Opening up the box, I discovered there was what looked like very expensive jewelry in it. I touched the box, but didn't touch any of the jewelry. There were four gorgeous necklaces with emeralds and diamonds in them, three large diamond rings, two watches and some old coins.

My first thought was to call Shirley, but then my better judgment took over and persuaded me not to. It wasn't any of my business, and I didn't want any problem with Crystal because of the baby. I assumed, of course, the jewelry and coins had been stolen. I pulled out the bottom of my blouse from my slacks and wiped my fingerprints off the box and put it back under the seat. I opened a door and ran back to the trailer getting wet.

Chapter 42

SHIRLEY CALLED TO let me know she was going to the hospital (she said she had flowers for Crystal) and that she would be back soon after the visit- maybe about 8 p.m.

I was tired, but did some cleaning in the trailer, and then ordered pizza. When Shirley got home, I told her I had called the Hamiltons and told her that they had gifts for the baby. Shirley thought that was very nice. So did I.

Shirley said the baby was doing fine, and that the hospital had him on Similac. Crystal was in a foul mood and had talked ugly to the nurses. Shirley said Crystal mentioned the A word. Adoption!

Chapter 43

THE FOLLOWING MORNING, I didn't wake up until 10a.m. I could hear Shirley moving around the kitchen. Something smelled so good! She was making breakfast; orange juice, coffee, English muffins, eggs, and bacon. I quickly put my clothes on, walked into the kitchen and said good morning to her. We sat down at the kitchen table and thanked God for the food, and then we ate.

Being owner of the supper club, Shirley could decide when she was, or was not needed at the restaurant. Today, she was not going into work, but was going to the hospital to see Crystal and baby Gary.

While clearing off the kitchen table, I asked Shirley if they call their home a trailer or a mobile home. She laughed. "Either one is correct," she said. We usually just call it home.

Shirley was going to take pizza to the hospital for Crystal, but not beer. I thought that the reason Crystal was being so belligerent was due to her craving for alcohol.

After Shirley left for the hospital, I went out to Crystal's car and wrote down the make of the car and the license plate number. After finding the jewelry that was no doubt stolen, I wondered if the car also hadn't been stolen but I didn't want to get involved yet, anyway, because I couldn't risk getting Crystal angry with me because of the baby. If I betrayed her in any way, I believed she would never let me see the baby again.

Chapter 44

I WAS REALLY getting homesick; I began to question my motive for getting involved with Crystal and her family. What could this all lead to? What was this doing to me? Things just didn't feel right.

Chapter 45

CRYSTAL WAS DISCHARGED from Swedish medical on Saturday. Shirley brought her and the baby home. When I heard the car drive up, I opened the trailer door to help Crystal and the baby in, but Crystal drew back from me; however, when she got inside she handed Gary to me and then sat down on the sofa.

Shirley made three trips out to the car to bring in the gifts that the employees at the supper club had given her for the baby. There were also gifts from the ladies at Shirley's church. Shirley brought them all in and set them down on the living room table for Crystal to open when she felt like it. She told Crystal to make sure that the card would remain in the boxes each gift came in, so they could send thank you cards; I doubt very much if Crystal bothered to do that.

Gary was awake in my arms making sweet little baby sounds. He moved his little head slowly back and forth as if he was trying to figure out where he was. He looked directly into my eyes, and I was overwhelmed with emotion. I rocked him back and forth, as I held him in my arms, and then when he went back to sleep, I carried him back to his crib and laid him down on the pretty blue and white crib sheet and covered him with a soft Carter's blanket.

When Shirley went into the kitchen to get out a large pan to boil water in to sterilize the bottles, Crystal went to the fridge and got out a beer. After she guzzled it down, she looked relaxed. Not wanting to sit with her, I went back into the baby room to check on Gary, and to look at the shelves in the changing table to see if there was anything else we might need for him, but it looked like we had everything we needed for now, anyway.

I went into my bedroom and laid down to rest. Soon Gary would be hungry and would need his diaper changed. A few hours later, I heard the baby crying; I knew it was time for his bottle and a bath. When I walked into the kitchen to put the bottle in the warmer, Crystal walked up to me, but didn't offer to help.

"Jane," she said. "Remember, I want the baby called Harrison, not Gary like you have been calling him."

"I'm sorry. It won't happen again. I like the name Harrison," I said.

"Okay," she replied as she walked back into her bedroom.

Chapter 46

ONE EVENING, SHIRLEY'S mother called Shirley. She had made a definite decision not to renew her lease that was due by September 1st, and she would move in with them at that time to help with the baby. It wouldn't be long after that, the Emerson's new home would be ready for them to move into. I was relieved and distraught at the same time. If it was okay with the Emersons and Crystal, I would visit a few times a year.

Chapter 47

IT WAS THE last week in July. Remembering the promise I had made to the Hamiltons, I asked Crystal—this was on July 29th—if she would make sure she would be home to watch Harrison for about an hour the next day so I could go over the Hamilton's and pick up the presents they had gotten for Harrison. She assured me she would.

Crystal was home on the 30th to watch Harrison. Before I left, which was about 2 p.m., I fed and diapered the baby. He fell asleep, and I laid him in his crib. Driving away, I felt some apprehension about leaving Harrison with her, but I knew I wouldn't be gone very long.

After parking the car, I knocked on the Hamilton's front door; they seemed really happy to see me and they had a lot of questions about the baby and the Emersons. Mrs. Hamilton motioned for me to have a chair at the kitchen table where there was a large pan with homemade cinnamon rolls waiting for someone to eat them—and we did!

There were a lot of packages wrapped in blue and white for the baby, and also a stroller. Mrs. Hamilton asked me if he had a stroller, and she was pleased to know that he didn't; otherwise, she certainly would have taken this stroller back to the store. I was happy to see the stroller and anxious to put Harrison in it and take him outside for a walk.

I answered all their questions, and was honest about the way Crystal was acting. They were relieved when I told them that Shirley's mother was going to move in with them to take care of the baby, and that they would soon be in their new home.

Mr. Hamilton carried the packages and the stroller to my car and put them in the back seat. They made me promise to keep in touch with them. They waved as I drove off, and I thought to myself that they probably had tears in their eyes. This had not been a happy summer for any of us. I knew it had taken a toll on Mr. and Mrs. Hamilton. I hoped that soon they would call Shirley and go see Harrison.

Chapter 48

IT WAS ABOUT 3:30p.m. when I turned into the mobile home park and turned left onto the street where the Emersons lived.

"My God," I said out loud. "Crystal's car is gone!" My heart started pounding and I could hardly breathe. I pulled up to the fence (not shutting the car door) and ran to open the trailer door. Immediately, I heard Harrison screaming his head off. He was so upset, his face was red. He was sweating and was making choking sounds. Crystal had left him all alone, a little helpless baby all alone.

Carefully and lovingly, I picked him up and held him upright on my chest where he could feel my warm body against his. I walked him back and forth through the trailer and hummed him a song that my mother used to hum to me when I didn't want to go to sleep. He finally calmed down; I changed his diaper and gave him a bottle.

Oh, how I wanted to find Crystal and take wet mud and rub it in her face and all through her hair. I wanted to look in her eyes and call her every dirty name I could think of. Calm down, calm down, I told myself.

I was trapped. If I called the police, they might contact an agency that would place Harrison in foster care. If I called Shirley, she might confront Crystal, and Crystal would, no doubt, tell me to "get the hell out of Seattle and her life." But, something had to be done, and soon, for the sake of Harrison, no matter how much it would hurt me.

Chapter 49

SHIRLEY CAME HOME early, and was pleased to see the gifts that the Hamiltons had given the baby. She was really happy that they had given Crystal a stroller. Shirley said she would, personally, call the Hamiltons to thank them, and to let them know that they would be welcomed to visit Harrison at any time. I thought that was really nice of her.

That night, Don called Shirley. He called her often to check on how things were going, and told her that the job in Yakima was almost completed, and he planned to be home the next week. Shirley was glad, because they both knew he needed to go out to the new house to inspect the work that had been done and what they should do with the trailer.

Much to my surprise, Don asked to speak to me. He wanted to express his appreciation for my being there with his family during this difficult time in their lives and that I was to take the weekly checks Shirley had been leaving for me.

He asked me if I had heard the expression "Take the money and run," and that is what I was to do with the checks. Take them and use them. I hadn't cashed the checks, and wasn't yet sure if I would accept them or not. I had some of the money mom had sent me in my purse. Don had a great sense of humor I thought.

Each morning and afternoons, I took Harrison outside in his new stroller. We strolled up to the swimming pool one day, and the kids came up to the fence to see Harrison.

"Oh, how cute he is," they would say, or "He's so sweet." They wanted me to bring him back to the pool the next day!

Neither Shirley nor I had seen Crystal in days now. Things were much better when Crystal wasn't there. I had gotten so attached to Harrison, I dreaded the thought of having to leave him; I would just have to fly back to Seattle as often as I could to be with him.

Time to call dad again. First question, of course, was when I would be home and then Butch got on the phone and told me about this cute little female kitten Pup had found and brought up to the house. She had long hair. Her four paws were white and her chest was white and the rest of her was black. They named her Beauty because Butch said she was the prettiest cat he had ever seen.

After talking to Butch, dad got back on the phone, and asked about the baby. I started sobbing uncontrollably, as I poured my heart out to him: Crystal could care less about Harrison; the Emersons would soon be moving into their new home; a grandmother might be moving in with them to take care of the baby; and I didn't know how I could leave Harrison.

There was a long pause, as I cleared my throat and tried to compose myself. Dad didn't deserve hearing about my pain; he had enough of his own.

"I knew this would happen," he said. "That is why I didn't want you to go back there. Maybe what you need to do is to let the Emersons know you would like to fly back to Seattle now and then to see Harrison. I'll make sure you have the money to do this," he promised trying to cheer me up.

"Thanks dad. I would like that, and I'm sure the Emersons would too. I'll talk to them about it," I said as I wiped away my tears.

"Pet Beauty for me . . . and Pup too! I'm glad Pup found her. I know I will love her, and I love you too dad," I said.

"Oh, dad. Has Karl Helgens gotten out of jail on bond—I hope not, and do you know when his trial will be?" I asked.

Dad said that Karl was still in jail, and the trial had not been set as far as he knew. Karl's wife was in the process of selling their electrical business and had put her house up for sale. Dad thought she would leave town when her financial affairs were settled.

We then said our goodbyes, and I told him I would call him again soon.

Chapter 50

AUGUST ROLLED AROUND with dry and sunny long days. The temperature stayed about 75 degrees during the day and the nights were cool which made for good sleeping.

To help Shirley out, I made sure the trailer was clean, and the laundry washed, dried, and put away; and when Harrison was asleep, I did some cooking.

Harrison seemed to like our strolls around the trailer park, so we continued them; and now and then I would stroll him up by the pool to show him off. It was on one of those days after we had left the pool area that a car pulled up alongside of the stroller. It was Crystal and Buzz. My heart sank. I stopped pushing the stroller, and went up to her door to speak. She wanted me to dress Harrison in something cute and pack his diaper bag because she said Buzz's mother wanted to see the baby. I shuddered at the thought.

They slowly followed us to the trailer and waited until I changed Harrison's diaper, gave him some water from one of his bottles, and put a number of items in the diaper bag Mrs. Hamilton had given Crystal for the baby. I included all the bottles of Similac so he wouldn't get hungry. I didn't want them to take him, but there was nothing I could do.

Before they left, I asked Crystal if she would leave Buzz's mother's telephone number. She pulled out a napkin from the glove compartment and wrote down his mother's address, telephone number and her name and gave it to me. I thanked her and then asked her when Harrison was to see his pediatrician. She said she didn't know, but to ask her mother.

I kissed Harrison on his cheek as I gently handed him to Buzz since Crystal was driving. Crystal said they would have Harrison back by 8 p.m.

Chapter 51

THE STOVE CLOCK said 8 p.m., then 9 p.m., then 10 p.m. Shirley and I tried to watch t.v. and assure each other that Harrison was alright. We paced the floor until we were both so tired, we could hardly walk. I knew Shirley was as worried as I was. If I slept any that night it sure wasn't for very long. I could hear Shirley during the night talking in her sleep and now and then getting up out of bed; maybe to get something to drink to help her sleep. Maybe she was deciding whether she should take a sedative.

Shirley didn't go to work the next day—she was too upset. We talked about what, if anything, we could do. She decided not to call Don because he was due home later that afternoon or in the evening; she didn't want to get him upset while he would be driving, and there wasn't anything he could do on the road anyway.

Finally, after calling the number Crystal had given me on the napkin, a woman answered the phone. It was about 4 p.m. Shirley had called this time.

"Hello," an elderly sounding voice answered slowly.

"Hello, I'm Shirley Emerson, Crystal's mother. Is she there—I'd like to speak to her," Shirley asked hopefully.

"Who?" the woman asked.

"Shirley Emerson, the baby's grandmother," Shirley said somewhat louder.

"Oh yes, Harrison, the baby," she replied. "No, she isn't here, but she was here with Buzz."

"Did she say when they would be back?" Shirley asked.

"They told me they would be back later tonight," she said. "I hope it's not too late. I go to bed early."

Shirley asked her if she would write down the telephone number at the trailer and have Crystal call home the minute they got there. Shirley told her that it was very important that she calls. The woman—Buzz's mother—said that she would tell her. Shirley, disappointed that Crystal wasn't there, said goodbye and hung up.

We drove around the area for an hour or more hoping to see the car that Crystal had been driving, but I think we both knew, it was a waste of time. too big a city and too many cars. I felt emotionally drained. When we got back to the trailer, Shirley gave me a mild sedative and made me lay down.

Chapter 52

ABOUT 8 P.M. we heard a car outside and could see the headlights shining in the window. Hoping it was Don, Shirley rushed to the door to open it, and ran out to see that it was Don in his truck. Don got out, and before he could shut the door, Shirley was in his arms. He held her tight and they kissed. Then they walked to the trailer; Don had his arm around her waist.

Don was glad to be home I could tell. He look tired, but handsome in his work clothes; blue jeans, a red and green checkered shirt, boots and a cap. He took off his cap, spoke to me and smiled.

When they sat down to talk, I excused myself, but Don and Shirley both wanted me to share in their conversation. Don carefully and patiently listened to everything we told him about how Crystal was neglecting the baby—that she was seldom home; that Shirley's mother said she would come to take care of the baby; and how worried she was that a state agency might take Harrison away from Crystal.

Don sat, saying nothing for a while. He got up and walked into the kitchen for a Pepsi.

"Ladies," Don retorted as he talked between gulps, "I know who can help us." He began to walk over to the phone. He seemed jovial.

"Shirley, you remember my college roommate, Stuart Worthington?" He is a partner at Walsh, Brittan, and White. I'll call him right now and set up an appointment with him. I should have thought to do this sooner," Don said.

Chapter 53

JUST AS DON was about to pick up the telephone to call his attorney friend, we heard a heavy knock on the door. Don walked over to the door and opened it; there were two police officers standing side-by-side looking up at him.

They introduced themselves and asked if they could come in. One of the officers was awkwardly cradling a baby, and trying to hold on to a diaper bag.

"Oh, my God," Shirley cried. "Come in, come in."

"Are you Mr. and Mrs. Emerson?" one of the officers asked.

In unison, Don and Shirley answered, "Yes, we are."

"Is this baby your grandson?" the other officer asked.

"Yes, Shirley said as she looked at Harrison. The officer gently handed Harrison to her and put the diaper bag down on the floor. He looked relieved!

"Please come in and sit down, Officers," Don requested.

Harrison was quiet and sucking a thumb. Shirley and I took him back to his bedroom to see if he needed changing, and we wanted to look his little body over to make sure he was not hurt. He seemed alright, I went to the kitchen to prepare him a bottle.

"Where is Crystal, our daughter?" Shirley asked. Where did you find Harrison?"

"She and her friend, Buzz Hunt, have been taken to jail", the tall Officer Winter replied. "We apprehended them while they were robbing a pawnshop, and we believe they have robbed before. Now we have fingerprints that will determine it."

Shirley came back into the living room.

"How did you know they were in the pawnshop?" Shirley asked.

Officer Hunt answered. "We got a call on our radio that a man walking his dog noticed two figures inside the shop as he looked into the window. The man knew the pawnshop owner, and he knew the owner was out of town, so he went to a phone booth and called the station. We were there within a few minutes."

"What happened to your cheek, Officer Hunt?" Shirley asked.

"Your daughter—he chuckled just slightly—was quick. She threw a wrench at me before I could handcuff her."

"I think you'll need a couple of stitches," Shirley said. He nodded.

"I'm sorry to have to tell you this," Officer Hunt said," but it was the man, Buzz that told us about the baby and where he was. Handcuffed, they led us to the car they were driving—which by the way was stolen—and Buzz unlocked the door. The baby was in a clothes basket in the back seat. The car has been impounded".

"Mr. Emerson, your daughter is in a lot of trouble. Do you have an attorney?" Officer Winter asked.

"Yes, I do. In fact, I was going to call him before you came. I'm going to make an appointment with him," Don replied.

The officers left their cards. We thanked them, walked them to the door and said goodbye.

Chapter 54

THREE DAYS LATER, I was permitted to visit Crystal at the jail. A short, stocky female guard with rough complexion stayed in the room with us as we talked on the phone. There were eight or nine prisoners on the phones. Crystal was on one side of the plastic barrier, and I was on the other side.

"Hi Crystal," I said after we had the phones up to our ears. "I'm sorry it had to come to this."

"Me too," she sighed. "Buzz said we wouldn't get caught; that we would be rich and live in Mexico. I have told the investigators where we hid the money and the jewelry, but I don't know where Buzz got the car."

"Have you talked with your attorney, Mr. Worthington, yet?" I asked.

"Yes, he was here yesterday," she replied.

"Crystal, you know I like you and consider you a friend," I lied. "Would you let me take Harrison with me to Iowa to care for him until you get out of jail?" "I will sign legal papers stating that I would bring him back here when you would be allowed to see Harrison. He would be well taken care of. You know your parents have demanding careers, and your grandmother is really too old to raise a child. Butch, his grandfather, my dad, and I would take him to church and he would go to a good school. We have a dog and a cat, and as he gets older, I know he would love them."

"I guess that is a good idea if mom and dad think so too," she said. "I know he can't be in here with me," she softly chuckled.

"I'll talk to your parents about it and see what they think. We would have to get an attorney to make sure everything would be legal. I wouldn't want to be accused by anyone of kidnapping Harrison," I said.

"Is there anything I can bring you: books, snacks, magazines . . . ?"

"Mom is going to find out about that," Crystal said.

Our time was up. The guard came over; Crystal got up, said goodbye, and walked back to the door with the guard. I was glad to get out of that place.

I needed to talk to Don and Shirley about our conversation, and if they approved, I would call dad and Butch to tell them I would be bringing Harrison back with me and give them time to buy a crib and some other items the baby would need until I could shop for him.

After the Emersons and I discussed Harrison's future (we talked for two hours) they approved that it would be better for Harrison to be with me, dad and Harrison's grandpa, Butch. They could visit Harrison whenever they wanted to, and I would make sure Harrison visited them in Seattle. One thing that pleased them was that I told them that one day, Harrison would inherit Stormy Acres and that here was no mortgage on the farm.

Don said he would ship all of Harrison's belongings, including the furniture, to the farm. In the meantime, I knew I could borrow a crib.

Chapter 55

THE ATTORNEY THAT Don's attorney recommended to represent me, prepared all the papers needed for Crystal and me to sign, which we did. He was also very emphatic about Butch adopting Harrison within six months, so that Crystal could never try to take him away from us. I knew Butch would oblige wholeheartedly. No problem there.

When I was alone, I called dad and Butch, hoping they would be as happy as I was. I felt they were in a state of shock when I told them Harrison would be coming home with me, but I knew they were happy too.

Chapter 56

After Harrison and I boarded the big United Airlines plane, found our seat and got comfy, I saw the Emersons waving. I waved back, but couldn't tell for sure if they could see me. The big fluffy clouds amazed me. I was gazing out in wonder at them when a stewardess bent over to look at Harrison.

"Your baby is adorable," the pretty young woman said with a loving smile.

"Thank you—thank you," I replied joyfully.

Then I whispered in Harrison's ear, "Your dad would be so happy. He loves us both."

The End

By: Tamara Eden Huie 2010

Epilogue

WITHIN A YEAR after Gary Harrison Benson and I returned to Monticello from Seattle, Butch legally adopted his grandson. Butch has sugar diabetes, and doesn't see well, but he is still very active and enjoys being with Harrison. Dad lived to see Harrison's seventeenth birthday. He raced only two summers after Sharon's death. He spent his time bowling, farming, and teaching Harrison everything he knew about farming. Mom loves New York and Europe. She keeps in touch and sends money! Mr. Boorman and his family still live on their farm next to ours. Mr. Boorman is deaf. Son, Jeff, helps his dad on the farm, and does tax returns. Son, Mark, writes insurance, is married and helps on the farm. Mrs. Boorman is in poor health, and has a nurse who tends to her. The Emersons are still in their home bordering the championship golf course. They are retired, and both play golf. They have been to Stormy Acres a number of times to see Harrison. They love our livestock and our beautiful countryside, but I don't think they could ever adjust to country living or to the aroma the animals share with us! They gave their mobile home to their church. Crystal Emerson eventually was released from a Correctional Facility, but no one has heard from her since. Buzz: who knows! The Hamiltons keep in touch. They have moved into an Assisted Living Home. Karl Helgens was sentenced to life in prison without parole. Mrs. Helgens (Lauren) sold the electrical business and her home, and moved to California where she has relatives. Gloria, Karl Helgens' lover and secretary stayed in town and married Karl's first cousin who is a dentist. Jim Kaponi probably still plays pool, dabs in drugs and drives women crazy. Sheriff Wilson retired, and moved to Texas after a nice farewell party given him by the citizens of Monticello. He will be missed for a long time. We assume that Officer Hunt saw a doctor and had stitches put in his cheek. Kimi and Madison are married to prosperous local farmers and have children. Faren is married to an attorney, and works at John McDonald Hospital in town. She is an R.N. and has a daughter. Katie Mary is married to an M.D. and teaches physics at the High School. Shirley's mother DID renew her lease—and only <u>visits</u> Shirley and Don. Pup and Beauty are buried at Stormy Acres where the lily-of-the-valleys grow.

Jane Ahlrichs

Edwards Brothers,Inc!
Thorofare, NJ 08086
22 March, 2011
BA2011081